Aster

A Monster FFF Romance

Sofia Rose

Other Books by Sofia

SOFIA ROSE

<u>Fortune Records Omegaverse:</u>

Snapdragon

Aster

Iris

Zinnia

Fritillaria

<u>Briar Hill Omegaverse:</u>

Touched & Tamed

<u>Whimsywood Tales:</u>

A Teacup for Trouble

The Zodiac Society:

Patreon exclusive, 13 novellas

A Note on Omegaverse

Before you begin, I wanted to take a moment to explain the version of omegaverse you'll find in this series.

Omegaverse is a romance subgenre that originated in fanfiction spaces and has since evolved into many different interpretations across books and authors. There is no single "correct" version. What follows is *my* take on omegaverse, and the rules that apply specifically to the world of the *Fortune Records Omegaverse*.

In this universe, society is divided between humans and monsters, who have historically lived apart. Because of this separation, humans do not grow up knowing about omegaverse dynamics. Human characters are unaware of secondary genders, heats, mating bonds, and related biology until they spend meaningful time with monsters. For humans, a dormant secondary gender is only triggered through meeting a monster mate.

Secondary Genders

In addition to primary sex, characters in this world have a secondary gender: **alpha** or **omega**. Any primary gender can be alphas or omegas. There are **no betas** in this universe.

Among monsters, secondary gender can be sensed instinctively. Humans do not have this ability in the same way, though some humans may experience a faint or inconsistent awareness of a mate. Monsters, particularly shifters, have heightened senses of smell, which makes their ability to scent secondary gender and mates far stronger and more reliable.

Omegas are not publicly labeled or categorized within human society.

Scent

Both alphas and omegas have distinct, unique scents, often influenced by personality, emotional state, and individual biology. A mate's scent is instinctively recognizable and often irresistible, creating a powerful pull between bonded partners.

When an omega becomes aroused, their scent sweetens, intensifying attraction and instinctual responses in nearby alphas. Scent plays a central role in attraction, bonding, and recognition throughout this world.

Heats and Instinct

Omegas experience heats, which are biological periods marked by heightened desire, sensitivity, and instinct. These urges often begin as an intensification of emotion and attraction, and can escalate into overwhelming instinct while in heat. Choice and consent still exist, but biology plays a powerful role in shaping how these experiences feel and unfold.

Mates and Bonds

Omegaverse bonds in this world are biological and deeply rooted in instinct. An omega will only ever be bonded to one alpha, and may also bond with additional omega mates within the same bond structure.

To complete a bond, two things must occur: a verbal acceptance of the bond, and a **claiming bite** from the alpha. The bite itself is pleasurable for the omega and marks the bond as fully formed. Until both acceptance and the bite occur, the bond remains incomplete.

Anatomy and Knotting

Male alphas in this universe have knots as part of their anatomy. A knot is an expanding ring of tissue around the base of an alpha's penis that swells during orgasm. This is a biological trait associated with mating and bonding.

Pack Structure

Pack dynamics in this world consist of one alpha with one or more omegas. These dynamics are instinctual rather than societal, and individual relationships may look very different depending on the characters involved.

This note is not meant to be exhaustive, but rather to offer grounding before you begin. As with all omegaverse stories, much of how these elements function is revealed through character experience, emotion, and connection.

Thank you for reading, and I hope you enjoy this world as much as I loved writing it.

Content Warning

The following book contains content that may be triggering for some readers. There are themes of segregation, coming out, and internalized heterosexuality.

Content includes: dominant and submissive relationships, electro-stimulation, sexual awakening, coming out, sexual activity in the workplace, brat dynamic, tail play, horn play, wing play, nonhuman sexual activity, rope bondage, forced orgasm, pain as pleasure, mating bites, omegaverse.

If you need any more information on any of the above, you can email me at sofiaroseauthor@gmail.com

Aster is the second book in the Fortune Records series. For your own enjoyment, I would recommend reading Snapdragon, the first book, before reading Aster.

Aster takes place in a parallel time line to Snapdragon.

Dedication

For my wife.

And for anyone else who needed a queer story like this.

Chapter 1

H*yacinth*

Waking up at the crack of dawn was not what I expected from the music producer lifestyle. Hopefully that changes.

Today is my first day at my first real, big girl job. No internships here, I'm a fully fledged member of staff. Not only that, but it's with one of the biggest record labels in the city, Fortune Records.

It's all very last minute though, I got the call two days ago to ask if I wanted the job. Which I think means that someone else turned it down, but I'm not going to let that get to me. If I got offered the job, then I'm at least *one* of the people that they wanted.

Even though Fortune Records is one of the big ones, I'm not surprised that someone has turned them down. The label has always been a top place to work, at least until a few weeks ago.

Fortune Records became the first label to bridge the gap between humans and monsters. We don't mix, or at least we didn't until recently. But a few companies have been trying to diversify their audiences, and there is a definite shift happening in the space.

I'm going to be working as a sound tech for Flora, a newer singer in the industry. Her producer, Alex, is who I'm excited to work with though. I've admired their work this past year and I'm excited to get to know them.

Flora has reportedly been *dating* a Monster. I haven't really followed the news all that much on it, but I've seen a few pictures of them at events together. I wonder if I will meet him today, too.

As far as the monsters... I'm not against them or any-thing. But I also have no frame of reference. There's not much online that's helpful and I'm not sure what to ex-pect. Fortune Records opened their new studios for both humans and monsters, right between the two territories. That's where I'm going to be working. It's nerve racking, but also really exciting. I think I'm just more curious than anything.

I yawn, moving through the motions of getting ready. A granola bar is all I can stomach at this time of the morning, but I need something to go with my coffee.

Opening the fridge, I see the lunch that Riley has packed for me. He is an absolute gem, Samantha and I give him money for groceries each week, and he kills it in the kitchen for us. I take out my green, frog printed lunch box and set it on the kitchen counter.

Our house is nice, and that's all down to Riley too. His parents own this place, and Samantha and I each rent a room. We all met in freshman year of college, and the three of us got this house the year after. Samantha and I are lucky that Riley adopted us. We were always the first ones in the library in the morning, and the last ones to leave at night, so we formed a quick study group turned friendship. Three years have gone quick here, but my room definitely looks like it's been lived in longer than that.

I'm pretty proud of my little space, even though it's the smallest room. It's cozy, and I have everything I need. Especially Alfred, I place his freshly cleaned and filled water dish into the vivarium. His little yellow and brown body is huddled underneath the orchid, snoozing away. Hourglass frogs are usually active at night, so he won't miss me much today. I admire the little purple mushrooms that Samantha 3D printed for me, or for Alfred, I guess. They're the cutest little addition to his home.

I at least had the forethought to pick out an outfit last night. What do you even wear to a studio filled with monsters? Short answer, I had no idea. I decided to go for something modest, but with a little of my style. Slipping on my Mary Jane's, I wonder if these shoes might be a mistake. My commute includes a twenty minute walk when I get off, because no buses even go to that part of town. I'm thinking I can slowly dress more casual as time goes on in the job. And hopefully start my day much later.

My curly hair is a mess, as usual, so I throw it into my standard space buns.

When my satchel is packed and ready to go, I leave a little early, rather than wait around and let my nerves get the better of me.

Chapter 2

Hyacinth

Of course I make an absolute fool of myself, trying to open the door to the studio building. I must have tried for two whole minutes before I realized there was a buzzer to press.

A clicking noise sounds and I try the door again, finally making my way through. My bus was delayed and I half walked, half ran to the studio. My feet are throbbing and I can feel my baby hairs sticking to my face with sweat. A woman with snakes for hair, and deep gray skin comes out of a room to meet me, clipboard in hand.

"That took you an embarrassing amount of time," she says in a bored tone.

"Oh," I tug on my dress. "You saw that?"

"Hmm..." She looks me up and down, disapproval in her stare.

If she could see me struggling with the door, I don't know why she didn't just come and open it. The woman is staring at me expectantly, her snakes squirming and looking at me from all angles.

"I'm Hyacinth Browne. It's my first day of work here." I try not to stare at her snakes, her form towering over me.

"I'll call Liliana. She is your buddy, her job is to help you settle into the company." The woman turns and strides into the room to the side. I awkwardly follow her and stand just inside the doorway of what appears to be some sort of reception area. I hope this Liliana person is much nicer than this woman.

"Just sit. Your hovering is annoying."

I perch on the edge of a seat as she picks up the phone and dials. The air conditioning is cooling me down a bit and I am finally starting to catch my breath. I'm not the outdoorsy type, and I've barely attempted exercise for the past year. I guess a twenty minute walk in heels was a bit beyond my abilities.

I'm too lost in my own thoughts to really notice what the woman says on the phone, but a few minutes later there's a knock on the door. I look up to see the most intimidating woman I have ever seen.

She is impressively tall, with a set of red and black wings rising high above her shoulders. A slim tail sticks out from behind her, and two black horns poking through her thick, deep red hair. She glances at the snake woman, and I notice that her ears are pointed and tipped with black.

I stand to attention at the authoritative shape that she cuts in her slim fitted suit. She may be intimidating, but she is also stunning. Her porcelain skin contrasts against her red and black tones, in an unnatural white. Her tail flicks casually as she takes in my appearance.

"Liliana," she holds a hand out to me, her fingernails black tipped claws.

Pleasure flows through me as I take her offered hand, and I nearly stumble from the force of it. I feel the sudden urge to want to please Liliana, to blindly do whatever she asks of me.

I shake my head, trying to clear my thoughts.

"I'm Hyacinth." I adjust the strap of my satchel, just to do something with my hands. I meet her stunning red eyes

as she smirks. The snake woman is forgotten as I follow
Liliana out the door.

Liliana

Hyacinth is much more adorable than I expected.

I've met tens of humans in the past two days since this
new branch opened, but none of them have had such an
impact as this one. She can't be much taller than five feet
without those shoes she's wearing.

Not much about the Humans I have met so far has
fascinated me quite like this. Hyacinth is delectable, her
skin, hair, and eyes all a rich, warm brown that seems to
glow from within. Her scent makes my mouth water, a
light citrusy clementine. I sneakily sniff the air as I turn to
look at her again. Yes, there's an underlying earthiness too,
like vetiver. Fresh and relaxing all at once.

I take in her appearance from the bottom up, starting at
those saintly Mary Janes with little frilly socks. She wears
a corduroy pinafore dress layered over a blouse, creating

the most delightful, innocent look. It makes me want to devour her. I wonder if she tastes as good as she smells.

I wasn't happy about having to spend my valuable time showing around a Human, teaching them the ropes. But the blush spreading over her cheekbones, highlighting those chestnut brown eyes makes me question my initial judgment.

Her eyes widen as a naga moves toward us, nodding his head in greeting.

"Liliana!" He enthusiastically holds out a hand to Hyacinth. "Is this our new sound tech?"

"I'm Hyacinth." Her voice is a high pitched chirp as she tries to hold in her surprise.

"Bring her around to my office later to sign some paperwork." Aspis tells me, humor lighting his eyes as he takes in her reaction to him.

"Of course." I reply.

I watch Hyacinth as she observes Aspis moving away, his snake-like tail trailing behind him.

"Not very hygienic." I tell her, checking my claws.

"No, I guess not," she giggles. "Sorry if I'm being weird, I've just—"

"You've never met a monster?" I cut in.

"Well, yeah." She toys with her bag again, a nervous tell of hers by now.

I find that I don't want her to be nervous or unsettled around me. I've never really had this sort of reaction to meeting someone before. Well, except…

"So, what's the plan for the day?" Her soft voice cuts through my thoughts, bringing me back to the present.

"I'll take you on a quick tour of the building. Then I'll take you to HR to do your induction and fill out the paperwork with Aspis."

Hyacinth

I almost lose my way to the break room, but the bright red door stands out as my saving grace. Liliana said she would meet me back here for lunch after she dropped me off with HR.

Part of my induction was learning about the different types of monsters we have in the studio. I'm not sure how much of the information that I will even remember, if I'm being honest. I ran out of available space in my brain pretty quickly. Which isn't like me, I normally want to be the best in the class, to force myself to remember everything.

I just couldn't help but be distracted by the orc female that helped me with my paperwork. Monsters were called females and males, I had learned. An easy fix in my language to make my new colleagues more comfortable. Her name was Tabitha, and her green skin wasn't as shocking now that I had met a few monsters, but it was her tusks that really fascinated me.

Nothing compares to Liliana though, I think, as I see her nod to me from across the break room. I find myself wondering what she looks like under that tailored suit, what other monstrous features she may be hiding under there.

She smiles at me warmly, and I ease myself into my chair. I learned in my HR induction that Liliana is a succubus, which is essentially a sex demon. Part of her powers includes being incredibly attractive, and giving those around her sexual pleasure.

That made me feel better when I learned that, my initial attraction to her explained. She probably can't help but have that effect on people.

Liliana chuckles when she sees my lunch box and I feel my cheeks warm, immediately self conscious. Maybe I needed a more professional setup?

"It's cute," she says. "It suits you perfectly."

Her bright, unnaturally red eyes meet mine, and I preen under her sort of compliment.

While I feel a bit more comfortable with Liliana now, she still sets me on edge a little. I struggle to keep up with the conversation as we eat, getting distracted by some new aspect of her appearance or behavior that I notice. Luckily, she seems to not mind, keeping the conversation flowing when I stumble.

Chapter 3

Hyacinth

Over lunch, I learned that Liliana works in PR for the label, coaching artists for the press, and running event campaigns. Once we're finished eating, Liliana finally takes me to meet Alex and Flora in the studio.

She leaves me at the door to make my own introductions. I knock and wait for someone to answer. After a minute or two, I knock again. I lean back, looking at the 'Recording in Progress' light, but it's not turned on. So I take a deep breath and open the door.

Alex is behind the mixing desk, they're wearing their headset over their copper hair as they watch Flora through the plexiglass. Flora is more beautiful in person, her golden hair bouncing as she pops up from bending behind the piano. Her mouth moves and Alex gives her a thumbs up.

Flora notices me first, waving and speaking quickly. I can't hear her on this side of the sound booth without a headset on like Alex's though.

Alex turns, taking off their headset and giving me their hand to shake.

"You must be Hyacinth!" Their friendly grin puts me at ease for the first time today.

"Yes. It's so nice to meet you." I shake their hand as Flora comes bounding out of the sound booth in a ball of energy.

She goes right in for a hug. "Welcome to the team!"

I enjoyed working mostly with monsters today, but I was slightly more on edge around them. I easily settle into chatting with Alex and Flora, the familiar space of a studio helping as well.

I mostly observe, as Alex and Flora work through some songs that she's writing. The studio is so high tech, and I want to learn how to use it to its full capability.

"Would I be allowed to come into the studio on my own to practice?" I ask as we settle onto the couch for a break.

"Yeah, of course!" Flora says, tucking her feet up underneath her and checking her phone.

"If you're having any trouble with someone saying you can't book a studio, just say that me or Flora told you to work on something and you should be good."

Flora and Alex are both so lovely, they ask me about myself for a few minutes before we get back to work. Flora being so nice also solidifies for me that the monsters can't be so bad if she's dating one of them.

"Oh, I almost forgot." Alex turns to me. "I'm meeting the coolest producer for coffee in a couple days. Are you up for joining?"

"Absolutely!" I have to stop myself from jumping in my seat. First day in the job and I'm already networking. "Who are they?"

"So you probably haven't heard of her. Her name is Addison, she produces for Sebastian, Flora's boyfriend. You should listen to Sebastian's music this evening and then you'll get excited to meet her." They nervously run a hand through their hair. "Trust me."

Wow. Addison must be really good if even Alex is nervous to meet her.

Chapter 4

Addison

It's the afternoon, and it still feels too early to be conversing with practical strangers. But I suck it up, Alex was so enthusiastic when I met them at the studio opening. I know that I should encourage that.

But ugh, why is it always coffee in a brightly lit space? I wanted to either be in the studio or in my house, not stuck in this bleak and sterile break room. Like, have they ever heard of mood lighting? I haven't been much of a fan of working in this new studio. Sebastian and I used to do a lot more of our work in privacy, at either his home or mine. The label has been pushing us to interact with the humans though. Not to mention, Sebastian is keen to be near Flora.

I'm also trying to make an attempt with Sebastian's human girlfriend. I'm meeting her producer, Alex, today. They texted to say that they were going to bring their new studio tech as well. Which was just the icing on top of the cake. The last thing I needed was to have to entertain a practical intern. Anything production related that I talk about will probably go over their head, anyway.

Alex holds open the door to the break room. An earthy, citrusy smell catching my attention immediately. The most stunning little human follows behind, a tray of coffee cups and a takeout bag balanced precariously in her hands.

I'm out of my seat before I realize what I am doing, taking the coffee cups from her to help her out. A light blush creeps across her cheeks and nose, her freckles standing out against her warm, brown skin.

I smile, sweeping a gaze over her ensemble. She's wearing mushroom printed overalls layered over a collared crop top. Her curly hair is tossed up into a matching pair of buns, sparkly clips pinning back her face framing pieces. Long, thick lashes brush against her cheekbones as her blush deepens under my inspection.

Realizing that I may be acting strangely, I say hello to Alex and wait for my introduction to this wonderful person.

"Hey, Addison. This is Hyacinth, I had mentioned that she might come along." Alex makes their way to the table I had vacated.

Instead of following, I look back to my little Hyacinth. "It's lovely to meet you. I can't wait to get to know you better."

This little human was going to be mine, I could feel it, and my witch's intuition was never wrong. I take the bag from her hands and bring the haul to the table. I look back to see Hyacinth still standing there, blinking quickly and giving her head the most adorable shake before moving to join us.

Alex starts to take the coffees from the tray, setting a pink takeout cup in front of me.

"This is from Rosie's café, she's Flora's best friend." They take a sip from their cup, eyes gently closing in pleasure. "Makes the best coffee in the human side of town. I got you something sweet and milky, I remembered you had mentioned having a sweet tooth."

"Thanks, Alex." That's cute that they remembered. My coffee is sickeningly sweet, a dark and rich caramel flavor countering the strong blend. Perfect.

"How do you take your coffee, Hyacinth?" I want to know everything there is to know about her. She blushes again, her head dipping lightly before she answers.

"I just graduated college, so I'm battling a raging coffee addiction. I take it black with some cinnamon and honey."

"I've never heard of that," I tell her. "Can I try a sip?"

"Yeah, of course!" Hyacinth holds out her cup to me. I make sure to brush my fingers against hers as I take the cup. I charge the touch with a slight spark of my electricity, one of my many talents as an electro witch.

I take a moment to sniff the brew, enjoying her scent mixing with the coffee. I just wanted to put my mouth somewhere hers had been so recently. I make a face as I take a sip though, the bitter coffee and burnt cinnamon not countered in the slightest by the honey.

"It's not for you." Hyacinth giggles, covering her mouth with her hand as she takes the cup back.

Immediately taking a sip from my own drink, I try to banish the awful taste coating my tongue. I'd do it again though to see Hyacinth's eyes light up with mischief.

"So you've just graduated?"

Alex rips open a bag of pastries and digs in as Hyacinth answers. I reach in and grab a flaking pastry drizzled in caramel.

"Well, I graduated a couple weeks ago, but I've been finished classes for over a month."

"She got Valedictorian." Alex cuts in, the sound muffled from their mouth full of pastry. So my little human is smart, too?

"Impressive. What did you study?" I ask her, resting my head on my hand and giving her my full attention.

"I was able to major in music production in my college. But I also got a minor in software engineering from all the extra classes I took in that."

She's perfect. Her stunning brown eyes search mine for validation and I try to give her a warm smile of encouragement.

"Then you'll be able to keep up while we talk shop." I wink at her and turn back to Alex, whom I'm just noticing that I've been mostly ignoring.

The purpose of our coffee was to meet up and let Alex pick my brain on some production issues they've been having.

I spend close to an hour helping them through their issues, scraps of paper littering the table with their notes. The whole time I am stealing glances of Hyacinth. She worries her bottom lip when she's thinking and it makes me want to lean in and kiss her. I hold back though, trying to keep my thoughts purely technical.

When we start to pack up our things, I take a minute to bring the conversation back to Hyacinth.

"How are you settling in with the company?"

"I'm really enjoying it!" She beams. "My buddy has been super helpful too. You might know her, she works in PR so I'm sure everyone does. Liliana?"

My heart stops as the movement in the room slows down around me. I need to concentrate on my breathing, taking a moment to calm down. Anyone but Liliana. My little human could have been paired off with anyone. My blood boils as I think about the things Liliana might say to my poor Hyacinth.

"I can speak to some people, get you a new buddy." I place my hand on her shoulder in sympathy.

"What?" Hyacinth's eyes widen in surprise. "No! I was saying that I like her. She's been really helpful with me settling in."

I'm confused. Is there another Liliana in PR all of a sudden?

"Oh, Hyacinth! Could you come up to the offices with me? I forgot that there was one last piece of paperwork to fill out." Tabitha calls out from the doorway.

"I guess I've got to go." Hyacinth looks to Alex, "I'll be right down to the studio when I'm done. It was great to meet you, Addison. I'll see you around!"

She flits out the door, clumsily catching herself mid stumble in her haste to follow Tabitha. Her innocence is breathtaking, but I worry that people like Liliana will take advantage of her.

Chapter 5

Hyacinth

I lean back in my gaming chair, absentmindedly moving through the levels of a game I've played hundreds of times. I wanted to play something that I didn't have to think about, something comforting.

Things have been going super well at work. Alex and Flora keep the strangest hours, never really starting work until late morning at the earliest. It suits me perfectly. I have plenty of time to relax first thing, either playing games or reading. Although, I have lost some of my evening time with Riley and Samantha.

That's why I'm excited for my day off today. It's a Saturday, so my friends will actually be free to spend time with me. Riley had mentioned something about going to lunch at this new restaurant he's heard about, but I'll be happy if we just stay home and get takeout too.

But for now, I can get lost in my thoughts. I'm listening to some of Sebastian and Addison's music today. It's crazy to me that I've met both of them in person now. Sebastian was a bit standoffish, but Addison was amazing.

She exudes a cool vibe that I could never pull off. She doesn't really look like a monster at first glance, until you realize that her features are all natural. Her hair isn't dyed that dark purple, and her violet eyes aren't colored contacts. She wears a lot of dark clothes and layered crystal necklaces.

Alex told me that they heard that she's a witch. I wonder what kind of cool spellwork she can do. Her music is a prime example of it, in any case. I haven't been able to figure out how she does certain things with her production. The easiest answer is magic, but I would still love to ask her about it. Maybe she could teach me... I'm probably getting way ahead of myself with that one though.

We haven't spoken again since that coffee a couple days ago, but I hope that will change. I hope I can work with her on a track someday.

I take a sip from my energy drink, the red and black branding reminding me of Liliana's coloring. Addison was pretty weird when I brought up Liliana with her, but she must have just misheard what I had said initially.

Liliana has been amazing. Any time I need some help, she is somehow there. Even yesterday, she helped me out with some equipment I was moving. She always just seems to be where I need her at the right time and place.

I'm startled from my thoughts as my door busts open, Samantha bounding in, her golden curls bouncing.

"Sam! I told you, you're gonna give Alfred a heart attack one day if you keep that up." I check on my tiny frog, who is as unbothered as ever, tucked under a leaf and fast asleep.

"Oh, he's fine!" She plops down on my bed and folds her legs up under herself. Her hair is expertly curled, far too put together for her usual look.

"Are you going out?" I ask, swiveling around to face her.

"We are! Riley mentioned that restaurant, remember?"

I groan, "Ugh. Are we really going?"

"Yeah, he had to make a reservation so we kind of have to go. But it's just lunch, so we can still come home and play games after." Samantha shrugs, "Come on, it'll be yummy."

I'll be going, there's no question of that. I'm just tired after being switched on all week. I let Samantha pick out an outfit for me from my closet, I never successfully follow dress codes when left to my own devices. My first day at the studio a perfect example of that.

She dresses me in a short, pleated pinafore dress. It's a deep green, and while I would normally layer it over something else, she's insisting that it looks way better on its own. It's hot out today, so I let it go and pair it with my black combat boots. I keep with my usual hairstyle, but I let Samantha pull down some face framing pieces, and layer gold necklaces on me.

"There!" Samantha says, clasping my last necklace in place. "Now do your makeup while I get ready. You're going to look so hot!"

I don't know why she cares about whether or not I look hot, but she's out the door before I can reply. Picking up my phone to play some music, I notice a notification to say that I have a new follower request.

My phone tumbles out of my hand and onto the desk when I see that the request is from Addison. I scramble to pick it up again, accepting the request and following her back immediately. Her account is on private too, so I'm going to have to wait for her to accept my request now.

It doesn't take me long to do my makeup normally, but I decide to put in a bit more effort this time. I add a second coat of mascara and layer up my blush and highlight so I glow. I consider taking a selfie. I want Addison to think that I'm cool, and if I'm posting photos going to places with friends on the weekend, that has to be cool, right?

Snapping a few selfies, I quickly follow Samantha's call. "Quick, come on. The Uber driver is waiting outside."

When we finally get into the car, I realize that we're missing one third of our trio.

"Where's Riley?" I ask.

Samantha waits for the car to start moving before replying, her voice shaky.

"Don't be mad, OK?"

"Why would I be mad?" I turn to fully face her in the seat next to mine.

"Riley isn't coming and I maybe set this up as a date for you with Nick's friend, Chris." She stumbles through her words, trying to get them out as quickly as possible.

I turn away, taking a deep breath to calm myself. I know that Samantha means well. Since she started dating Nick, she's been trying to set me up on dates too. I don't blame her, Riley is already studying pretty hard for law school, while Sam and I have a bit more free time now that we're working. She obviously feels guilty for leaving me alone when she hangs out with Nick.

"I've told you that I'm happy on my own," I tell her.

"I know! I know you have, but Chris is great, I promise. He's a couple years older than us, and he's a project engineer for a big pharmaceutical company. So he's smart too, and he's hot, Hyacinth!"

He sounds like someone my parents would love. A nice guy on a great career path in a respectable industry. I haven't had much success in the past with dating. I was usually too busy with school to really care enough, so I haven't ever found a guy I did care about enough to date.

"Maybe I might explore dating now that I have more free time," I sigh, giving my friend a reassuring smile. "I'll try to be open minded about it. But only if you promise to never ever surprise me with a date again."

"You got it!"

Chris is handsome, I think, as I look at him over my second cocktail. We've only just been served our food, so the alcohol is going to my head already. He's nerdy, but in an attractive way. His glasses have a trendy tortoiseshell frame and his tawny brown hair is artfully swooped back.

His bright blue eyes are pretty, and I could almost be attracted to him. Maybe. I can't help but notice how he's not as tall as Liliana, how she would tower over him. I think I'm just slow to warm up to new people sometimes.

"How's your food?" Chris asks me a bit awkwardly.

I look down at my untouched pasta, "it's great!" I finally take a bite and luckily it is pretty good. I stuff my face as he continues to talk. He's a bit cocky, in the way that I find most successful engineers can be, and he hardly asks me anything about myself. It's because of people like him that I exclusively refer to myself as a producer and never a sound engineer. Despite the fact that I am just as good at sound engineering.

The meal goes by quickly, and I am almost free to go home and get cozy. I wonder if Riley will be around this evening and if the three of us can play board games together.

"Do you guys wanna come back to ours and hang out?" Samantha chirps, her cheerful voice showing no recognition of my current state of anxiety.

When the Uber comes, Nick immediately takes the front seat and I am subjected to squeezing in between Sam and Chris.

"Don't forget your seatbelt." Chris leans over me, his hot breath over my face as he buckles me in. It's sweet, and I smile up at him, but my heart's not in it.

Luckily, everyone else in the car takes a moment to check their phones, so I do too. I try not to squeal as I see that Addison has accepted my follow request. I'm quickly disappointed though when I see that she barely posts. Her last addition was from over a year ago, some stacked Polaroids on a table. I zoom in to see that they're of her and Sebastian's band. They must be her friends outside of work too then.

I look up to see Chris glancing away quickly, his eyebrows raised. He doesn't say anything, but there's a slight shift in his demeanor.

That shift is a bit more prominent back at the house. Chris chooses to sit next to Nick on the couch, rather than join me on the love seat. I can't say I'm disappointed, there's just something about him that I can't get past. Besides, he definitely got weirded out when he saw me zooming in on a photo with a tentacled monster and a minotaur. I didn't have time for bigoted people in my life.

I excuse myself for the evening pretty quickly and decide to hang with Alfred instead.

Chapter 6

*A*ddison

I couldn't help but look up Hyacinth online earlier, requesting to follow her straight away. By the time I got to take a break, she had accepted.

There's a post from today, a selection of photos from a boozy lunch with friends, by the look of it. My little human is stunning, her pert boobs on display in her low cut dress.

I try not to physically cringe when I flip to the next photo. It's a group picture of Hyacinth and three others.

Except one of the men has their arms wrapped around her from behind, his chin resting on her shoulder.

Does she have a boyfriend?! I scroll through her other photos, but none have this man in them. I click back into the pictures from today, realizing now that this wasn't a group of friends. It was a double date.

"What's up with you?" Nereus asks as the guys make their way back into the studio.

"Me?" I shrug. "Nothing. I'm good."

Sebastian tosses me a soda and I fumble over catching it.

"Something has definitely spooked you." He says, amusement lighting up his eyes.

It's a distraction. Maddox snatches up my phone from the couch, clicking in to see what I was looking at.

"Hey," he says. "Doesn't she work here?"

Nereus lazily snatches the phone from Maddox with one of his tentacles. "Oh, she works with Flora, I think."

Sebastian is next to snatch the device. My head is in my hands at this point, just waiting for the moment to pass.

"This is Flora's sound tech..." Sebastian struggles with her name.

"It's Hyacinth. Now give me back my phone." I say, sharply.

Instead, Maddox takes the phone back. "She's pretty." He huffs, his septum piercing jostling with the movement. "You into her?"

His hoofs click against the floor as he moves to hand me back my phone.

"You know we're just kidding." Nereus adds, taking in my grumpy stare.

"If I was into her, I wouldn't be saying anything to you guys until I told her first."

"Leave her be. Let's get back to work." Sebastian grunts in his solid alpha voice. Myself and Maddox shut up quickly while Nereus chuckles, picking up his drumsticks and heading back into the sound booth.

It annoys me when my friends exercise their alpha abilities. Even though he means well, I don't like how I feel the need to obey. Judging by the look on Maddox's face, he doesn't much like it either. Being an omega can be tough, sometimes.

After work, my Dad calls to ask if I can come home tomorrow for a family dinner. I try to push back that I was planning on working.

"It's a *Sunday*, Addie." He clicks his tongue in disapproval and I can imagine the look on his face.

"OK, Dad." I sigh. "I'll come home for dinner. But I'm driving back up tomorrow night."

We say our goodbyes as I start the engine in my car, hanging up as soon as I can.

Dinner with my six sisters was going to be a lot. At least I could use the drive home as an excuse to leave early enough.

My family was proud of my success. But they didn't understand why I had to keep working so much. They didn't understand that I actually like what I do, that I like to keep weird hours and spend my time mostly alone.

Sunday was a family day for witches, it was when we came together as a group and strengthened our magic. I would have preferred being powerless over having to make the trek home as much as they wanted me to.

There's a lot of things I do that my family disapproves of.

Chapter 7

L*iliana*

I catch Hyacinth moving equipment on her own again in the hallway. She struggles under the weight of the amp that she's trying to shift.

"Oh, Liliana, hi!" She waves before wiping the sweat from her brow and getting back into position.

"No you don't." I say, placing my hands on her shoulders and gently maneuvering her to the side. "I've told you about moving your own equipment before."

"I know, I know. I'm in a building of big, strong monsters who would be happy to do the heavy lifting for me." She defiantly stands with her hands on her hips.

I try to rein myself in, wanting nothing more than to tame this little brat and have her writhing on the floor beneath me.

I have to move slow, I remind myself. This is all very new to Hyacinth, and I definitely don't want to push her away. That doesn't mean that I can't show off though. I easily lift the amp with one arm, resting it on my hip.

Hyacinth gulps as she watches me, and I can't help my self-satisfied smirk.

"Where to?" I ask.

"Oh, um, this way." Her voice has that nervous hitch that I love to coax from her. I leave some distance between us as I follow. She's wearing another set of adorable overalls, and her ass swaying back and forth in them is hypnotizing.

We make our way into Studio 1, and she shows me into the sound booth to set down the amp. I've seen more of the inside of a studio than I ever have since Hyacinth joined the label. It's certainly giving me a bigger appreciation for the production teams.

"Do you need help setting it up?" I ask.

"No! No, I've got it." She tucks her hair behind an ear, as she bends over to mess around with some wires. "I'm sure you have lots of more important things to do than follow me around."

In a way, she's right. I'm up to my eyes in prep for a launch party that's in less than two weeks. Plus, I'm training the crap out of the singer that the party is for. There's plenty else I could be doing, but I can't help wanting to be here and help out Hyacinth.

"Are you sure I'm not going to find you down another hallway lugging something else in a few minutes?"

She has the decency to look ashamed, her cheeks reddening as she looks up at me.

"Come on then," I gesture her to follow me. "What else do you need?"

Chapter 8

A*ddison*

My back aches, a telltale sign that I've been working for far too long. I take off my headset and yawn, stretching my arms up and arching my back. Just another hour or so and I should have this section finished, then I can finish up for the day.

I'm making a conscious effort to catch up on the work I missed yesterday. Sebastian is doing his own thing today so I can focus on some heavy production in peace.

The door cracks open slowly, a wash of my favorite clementine scent reaching me. Hyacinth is engrossed in her phone, so she doesn't spot me right away.

"Oh," she startles. Looking up, her eyes meet mine and I grin. "Sorry, I didn't mean to interrupt."

Hyacinth turns to leave. I'm out of my chair, hand on the door before I realize what I'm doing.

"You can stay, if you like." I tell her, slowly pushing the door closed when she doesn't resist. "Got any big technical problems that you're working through? I'd be happy to help."

My hand is still settled on the door, stretched over her head. She looks so small up close like this.

"Really?" My little Hyacinth looks up at me with her doe eyes, shielded by her fluttering lashes. If I didn't already know, now would be the time that I would see that I'm a goner.

"Yeah! Come on, sit down. My back needs a stretch anyway." I step back, allowing her to pass by and get settled.

"I'd rather see what you're working on, if I'm being honest."

"Oh, yeah. I can show you." I lean over her, playing what I have on the song so far.

"This is so cool," Hyacinth looks up at me, her chestnut eyes filled with excitement.

"What would you do here?" I point to a particular section on the monitor. She worries her bottom lip between her teeth as she concentrates.

"Can I?" She asks, gesturing to the mouse. I nod, backing off so she can work.

We go back and forth, and I coach her through why some choices wouldn't work. She does excellently, my little human is much better at all this than I was when I first left college.

I'm leaning over her, as I show her something particularly intricate. While I thought we were both concentrating hard, I notice the sweet underlying scent of Hyacinth's arousal. Her legs are closed tight together but the scent still reaches me.

Whether or not she has a boyfriend is still up for discussion, but my little human is definitely into me.

Chapter 9

Hyacinth

Addison hovers over me, not touching, but too close for comfort. It's so tempting to just lean into her. I want her to wrap me in her arms while I toy with her violet braids.

I thought that I was just admiring Addison, that I wanteded to be successful like her. But it's more than that, I realize now, as I look back to her. Her face is inches from mine as she bends over the desk, her focus on the screen. It's attraction that I feel.

I've never been interested in a woman like this before, or a female I guess in this case? I take a moment to truly look at Addison while her attention is not on me. She's tall, much bigger than me. While her form is slim but soft, and again I wonder what it would feel like for her arms to hold me. What would it feel like to rest my head against her soft boobs?

My panties are dampening, I realize as I quickly look back to the screen. Pressing my legs together, I try to subtly create some friction there.

I can't help but glance up to Addison again, only this time she's looking back at me. She turns my chair and settles her hands on the armrests, effectively caging me in. My breath comes out in little pants as she moves closer.

"Are you interested in me, little Hyacinth?" Her braid tickles my cheek as she whispers in my ear. A shiver winds its way through my body from the contact of her breath. My answer comes in the form of a desperate whimper.

No words will form, but I nod when she leans back to look at me. The violet in her eyes is much more pink up close, her lips more pouty.

Impatience gets the better of me. I lean forward and press my lips to hers, a gentle peck to gauge her reaction. That one tiny brush of our lips sends an electric current straight to my core.

My hands move to her neck of their own accord, just as Addison's meet my waist, pulling me out of the chair. She sits on the table and I slot between her legs, our bodies flush against one another and she deepens our kiss.

It's not gentle anymore. Her arms are around me now, her boobs pressed against my own, and it's so much better than I imagined. Addison's tongue teases at my lips and I let her in, completely submitting to her.

I lose myself for a moment, my body becoming a ca-cophony of sensations and my mind turning to mush. All I know is how good I feel kissing Addison.

Eventually, she pulls away. Her eyes meet mine as we share a secret smile. I giggle a little as I try to catch my breath. Addison holds my face in her hands, mine planted on her soft thighs.

Except I don't catch my breath. It speeds up further when I realize what we've just done. Addison must see the panic in my gaze, as she softly strokes my cheek.

"What's up?" She asks, her delicate tone almost calming me.

"I-I've never..." I gulp down some air, trying to finish my sentence. "I've never done that before."

"Hey, come here." Addison pulls me back toward her. "I've never kissed someone at work either. But I don't think anyone saw us, and besides, lots of people in here get up to—"

"No," I cut her off. "I've never..."

I toy with one of her necklaces, the leather cord soft against the pad of my thumb.

"You've never kissed a female before, have you?" She probes, getting out the words that I can't.

My nod is almost imperceptible, but Addison picks up the slight movement anyway.

"Oh, honey." Addison continues stroking my cheek soothingly. "That's OK. We all have to have our first time once. Just know, there's nothing wrong with you."

She pointedly looks in my eyes to make sure that I understand. I know there's nothing wrong with being attracted to any gender. I just didn't think that I was.

"I'll give you some space, if you need." Addison shifts to standing, separating our bodies. "I want to be clear with you though. I'm very much interested in you, Hyacinth. I want to see where this goes between us."

She kisses me again, a quick brush of our lips. It leaves me wanting more. But she's right, I need to take some space and process this.

"I-I'm interested in you t-too." I stumble over my words, forcing myself to push them out. I've never felt this way before, and I have no experience in expressing my feelings like this.

"You're right, though." I continue. "I just need to take some time to process."

"Take what you need." Addison's brow furrows in disappointment, but I can tell that she's trying to push through it for me.

I pull away from her, grabbing my bag and leaving the studio in a rush.

Once I'm in the hallway, the weight of everything hits me and my breath comes out in heavy pants. I race down the hall, eager to go home. I didn't even work on the project I was planning to, but I need to get out of here.

I turn the corner in a rush, and run smack into Liliana.

Chapter 10

Liliana

This studio party will be the death of me. It's not often that I come across a debut artist who has quite this level of audacity. Regardless, I have to push through and get it done. In less than two weeks, I will be free of this. Maybe I will take a week off work once it's all over.

I'm lost in my thoughts, walking towards the break room in search of my fifth coffee of the day. A bundle of brown curls quickly rounds the corner and I don't catch them in time. I realize a bit late that it's Hyacinth.

My joy at seeing her diminishes quickly when I attune to her senses. Her breath is coming fast and her little heartbeat is fluttering wildly.

"Woah," I steady her with my hands on her shoulders. I can tell by the panicked look in her eyes that she's not going to take in anything I say in this state. Looking around, I see an equipment storage room close by.

"Come on, this way." I take her hand and pull her into the storage room, flicking on the light as I close the door behind her. I gently coax her to sit on an amp before she faints.

"What's happened?" I ask as I brush her hair back from her face. It's rustled up, strands escaping her usual tidy buns. Her breath comes quicker. Fuck, she's on the verge of hyperventilating at this rate.

My protective instincts are screaming at me to do something, to calm her down.

I kneel before her so our faces are level with each other. Running my hands down her arms, I try to think of the best plan of action here. I can make her calm down with my powers, but I don't want to do it without her permission. Is she even in any fit state to give that though?

"I-I..." Hyacinth starts to speak. "I'm confused. I think..."

If someone has hurt my Hyacinth, I was going to do something that would get me in trouble.

"Shh," I continue stroking her arms. They're like icicles and I want to get some heat into her. "Go on. You can trust me."

She nods, seeming to come to some sort of conclusion.

"I think I like wome— females, I mean. Or both? No, not women." She scrunches up her face as she speaks, her breath calming some but not nearly enough. I needed to calm her down.

"What am I saying?" She shakes her head quickly. "I'm sorry, this is not professional. God, I'm failing at being in a proper job."

She pushes away from me, moving to stand. Swaying on her feet, Hyacinth nearly collapses from the movement. I catch her, moving her back to sitting on the amp.

"Not so quick, love." I tell her, going back to stroking her arms. "How about this? I've decided that I'm your friend outside of work. So now it's fine, we're friends, and you can talk to me about this. You don't need to worry about being professional with me. OK?"

All I want to do is help her calm down. Hyacinth nods, and I see her struggle to take in a deep breath. I fear she might be too far gone to calm down without my help now.

"Hyacinth? I can help you. I can use my powers to calm you down. But I need your permission to do that. Would that be OK with you?"

Her eyes widen, her breath coming faster again. What did I say?

"Have you— have you not always been using your powers?"

I'm affronted, and I can't help the scoff that leaves me. "I would *never.*"

Her heartbeat is speeding up some more now. Am I going to have to force this on her?

"Are you sure a little doesn't just seep out?" Her quiet plea confuses me. I don't understand what is going on in her head right now. But I need to use my powers.

"*Please.* Please let me help you."

Hyacinth nods. Finally.

I focus my mind and send an intention of calming energy to her. Keeping close attention to her heartbeat, I keep going until it returns to its normal pattern.

Fuck, that was close.

My head dips as I calm myself down too. God, it was tough to reign in my alpha instincts there. I never want to see her like that ever again.

Giving her my full attention, I wipe Hyacinth's tears away and offer to listen.

"I'm sorry," she sniffles. "I just... I've been attracted to some females in the studio and I just... I've never felt anything like this before. I thought I was straight, but I don't think I understood what it meant to be truly attracted to someone. But I've never been into human women..."

My poor Hyacinth. I wish she had come to me sooner, although why would she have? I've been holding back, giving her the space to come to me. This whole time I've been teasing her, confusing her. I should have been more open about my attraction to her from the beginning.

"Maybe you're not into human women then." I can't help but tuck a wayward strand of hair behind her ear, cupping her face softly. "Perhaps your tastes are more aligned to female monsters. And that's why you haven't been properly attracted to anyone else in the past."

"I'm really attracted to you." Hyacinth says, looking up at me with her doe eyes. "I thought it was just your powers. But it's not, is it?"

"Oh, baby girl." I grasp her chin. "I would never use my powers on you without asking, or having some sort of standing agreement first."

Hyacinth leans forward, gripping the lapels on my blazer, as her gaze focuses on my lips.

"Then why do I feel like this?" She asks, pressing her lips to mine.

I knew that I was attracted to Hyacinth, but nothing prepared me for this feeling. Her tiny, fragile form clinging to me as she tries to deepen our kiss. My desire to protect her in this moment wins out, though.

I delicately extract us a bit. "Love, I would like nothing more than to kiss you right now. But you've just been through a lot, and I never want you to regret me."

I'm so confused by what I am feeling right now. This protectiveness, this need to love and hold this little human. But I can't sense any kind of mating bond. I needed to call my parents.

"You've been through a lot today." I stand up, holding Hyacinth as she rises as well, making sure she is steady on her feet before I let go. "How about I drive you home?"

Chapter 11

Hyacinth

The drive home is quick. Sickeningly so, considering how long my bus and walk commute normally takes me. I really needed to get a car. And learn to drive.

My eyes track every tiny movement that Liliana does. My breath catching when I watch her confidently switch gears. Since when did driving become so attractive?

She seems so comfortable and self assured. I know she is older than me, but I don't think that aging was going to ever give me that level of confidence. I just want to lean into her for support, to have her take care of me.

"You doing OK?" she asks, turning on to my street.

"I'm much better now." I unbuckle my seat belt, turning to face her when we pull to a stop outside my house. "Thank you."

"Of course." Liliana reaches over, cupping my jaw with her hand. "You can talk to me whenever you need."

Once I'm at the door, I turn to see her still watching me. I think she's waiting to make sure that I get in OK. Closing the door behind me, I rest my head against it.

Liliana's magic helped to calm me, and I'm grateful for that. I finally have the clarity of mind to sort through my thoughts properly. God, I am a piece of shit, stringing along both Liliana and Addison.

Fuck, I kissed them *both*.

Since when do I do that?

Am I supposed to choose between them? Liliana is so strong and supportive, but Addison understands my work and she is so soft and caring. No, I refuse to go down this train of thought.

But fuck, they're both females. Not only do I now apparently have a thing for my own sex, but it's monsters on top of that.

There's absolutely nothing wrong with being queer. I know that. I just didn't expect this of myself.

I think back to that stupid date with Chris at the weekend. I could recognize that he was attractive, and I appreciated that he was a catch, for *someone*.

How have I been so blind?

No wonder I've never really enjoyed sex. Kissing Addison and Liliana today... I felt more with them in just a simple kiss than I ever did with a guy. Fuck, just a touch from one of them sent goosebumps running down my spine.

Sex has always been such a 'tick box' exercise for me with past partners. What would sex be like with a female?

At least both Addison and Liliana seem comfortable with giving me space to sort things out for now. I need that.

"Why are you just hanging out in the hallway?!" Riley pops his head out of the kitchen doorway. "Oh fuck, what happened to you?"

Crap. I definitely look worse than I thought.

"It's a long story..." I follow him into the room. "Tell you about it over dinner?"

"Of course, babe." He kisses my forehead, pulling me into a side hug. "Why don't you get comfy? Dinner will be ready in fifteen. My instincts said something comforting was in order. I'm making Cacciatore."

"I love you. Have I ever told you that?"

"Only when I'm cooking for you!" He smacks my ass, gesturing me towards my room.

I get changed into a satin short set and put on my coziest socks. I have enough time to set the table too, Samantha getting home just early enough to eat with us.

I tell them about my day, hardly leaving out a detail. Samantha and Riley both let me speak, even though I can tell they both want to jump in with questions.

"You can speak now," I chuckle.

"Oh, Cinthi." Samantha uses my nickname from Freshman year, before I decided it was too young for me. "I am so sorry for pushing you into that date at the weekend."

"No, it's OK. I needed a recent experience to compare this all to, I'm sure."

"No, it's not OK." Riley gives Samantha a look, having made his opinion on the matter pretty clear yesterday. She has the good sense to look ashamed. "But I don't think being sorry is going to help in this case."

I'm glad I have Riley. He's been through this before, coming out to me and Samantha back in Sophomore year.

"I'm happy for you, Hyacinth." He means it too, smiling at me and holding my hand across the table.

"Wait, this is a good thing..." My giggle sounds a little crazy, but Riley is correct. "I forgot about how this is actually a good thing."

"You betcha!" Samantha chimes in. "Just think about all the hot girls you're going to bring home."

"Females."

"Yes, females. Damn. Wait, do you have pics? I wanna see these monsters!" Samantha claps her hands, already making a game out of things. It's cute though, and she's right that I would want to gush over Liliana and Addison.

"I have Addison on social media, but I'm going to have to deep dive the label's material to find a good shot of Liliana."

I flick onto my social media app, opening Addison's profile. I pass the phone to Samantha, and Riley moves behind her to look in.

"Shit. She's hot," Samantha scrolls for a minute before I snatch the phone back.

"Let me find Liliana."

It takes me a couple minutes, but I find a headshot on the label's website under the info for the PR team.

"Oh wow, hello Mommy." This time Riley has something to say. "She looks scary. But in the way that I would thank her for killing me."

I burst out in laughter. "Why does everyone think Liliana is mean?"

"Babe, she looks like she would delight in death. Don't get me wrong, it's super hot. Her horns are super cool too."

I can't help but chuckle to myself throughout the evening as I think on that. We have a cozy night in, playing board games and chatting. My minor freak out temporarily forgotten.

Chapter 12

L*iliana*

"Call Dad." I tell my voice command system as I pull away from Hyacinth's house.

"Hey, honey." His cheerful tone comes across the speakers.

"Oh, Dad." My voice betrays my feelings, and I try to focus on the road as I head home. "I need your help."

"What's up? Did something happen?" He switches to serious immediately, his demon persona getting in gear. "Who do I have to hurt?"

"No, you don't have to hurt anyone, Dad. I just have a bit of a relationship dilemma and I need some advice."

"Has Hell frozen over? Or has my only daughter come to me for relationship advice? Both are as likely."

I make a mock sound of laughter. "Very funny, Dad."

Keeping a careful eye on the road, I turn on to the highway.

"How can I help?"

"I met someone."

"That's great, honey. When do we get to meet her?" He sounds genuinely delighted with that news.

"She's a human..."

There's a long pause, almost long enough that I think that the call might have dropped.

"Well, that's... that's OK, I guess." I can almost picture him scratching at his head, unsure of what to say. "I'm not sure I'm going to be much help for advice in wooing a human, honey."

"It's not that, Dad. Actually, please kill me if I ever come to you for help with wooing anyone." His chuckle grounds me. It seems he got over the human aspect pretty quickly.

"How did you know you and Mom were mates?" I ask, my voice soft.

"Well, it's physical. That's the first thing you should know. You feel a pull to your mate, an innate need to protect them. But most importantly, it feels right, you feel *complete*."

He pauses a moment before continuing. "I think if you had met your mate, you wouldn't be asking me this. Just if I'm being honest, honey."

I sigh, and my disappointment must be audible.

"I feel all this, Dad. But it feels like something is missing. I don't know what."

"Unless," he adds, "unless you're not complete as a pair."

Not complete as a pair?

That might actually make sense. Plenty of mates are trios, in rarer cases they can be four or five Monsters.

"Is she definitely an omega?" He asks.

"She's a human, Dad." I think back to her delicious scent though, how it was soured with her distress earlier. "Although she does have an omega scent."

"And you can smell it?"

I nod, then verbally agree when I remember that he can't see me.

"Honey, you're pretty unlikely to smell an omega's scent if they're not your mate."

"Wait, really?" I didn't know that. "Fuck. I have a mate."

"You've probably got *mates*." I hear him moving on the other end of the line, a rustling sound. "I'm so happy for you, honey. Can I tell your Mom?"

"Don't even pretend that you're not standing next to her right now."

The muffled sound of voices clues me in that Dad has covered the microphone on the phone with his hand.

"Oh, we're so happy for you Lili!" My Mom's voice carries into my car. "When can we meet them? I can have dinner this weekend at the house."

"Mom, thank you. But it's going to be a while before you can meet anyone. I have a lot to figure out."

I turn into my building's parking lot, cutting out the engine.

Chapter 13

I've learned a lot since that walk to the studio on my first day. Firstly, sneakers are the commuters best friend. Secondly, leave extra early and listen to music as you stroll.

No running here.

My phone buzzes in my pocket. I slip it out, it's probably Riley informing me that I forgot some element of my lunch today. I got a similar text the other day. Apparently, I was supposed to immediately know that the other container in the fridge was for me.

It's not a number I recognize.

I'm out with a client today, so you won't see me around. But I was wondering if you would consider letting me take you to dinner tonight? I can pick you up from the studio once you're finished work. Liliana

x

Of course she texts in full sentences like that. A shiver of excitement flushes through me, but I also feel a little dread. I don't know if I should really be pursuing either Liliana or Addison while I'm figuring things out.

Another text pops up in the chat.

It can be more so as friends, if you'd like.

Impulsively, I text her back. Letting her know that I'll go, I don't confirm if it's as friends or as a date.

I look down at my absolutely not dinner date appropriate outfit. Great.

Well, I guess this is what I'm stuck with.

The first part of my work day went by too fast. I hardly focused on my work, my mind straying to my two females. Imagining them in my mind's eye, remembering our kisses.

I wonder if I will get a second shot at my first kiss with Liliana tonight.

I head to the break room in search of coffee, leaving Alex and Flora to hang out on their own for a while. They're both super kind, but sometimes I feel like kind of a third wheel. They have been friends for years, so I totally get it. The small bit of peace is nice though.

The coffee machine is atrocious in this break room. You would think they would have invested in a better contraption in a studio filled with tired and overworked musicians. It slowly drips out my coffee, while also making the loudest crunching sound.

The machine is so loud that I almost don't notice a group coming into the space. I see Sebastian and his two band members. The tentacled guy grabs them all sodas from the fridge and places them on the table. I count four sodas and I hold my breath, hoping that Addison is going to join them.

She strolls into the room, her deep purple hair worn down, the pin straight strands catching the light in a dazzling shine. I quickly look away, pretending not to notice her. I don't want to come on too strong.

Addison's friends are loud and boisterous, reminiscing about a story from one of their tours.

"Hey," I look up to see Addison leaning against the counter next to me.

I can feel the blush warming my cheeks at her attention. I didn't think she would approach me in front of her friends.

"Hi," I cringe, my voice coming out as a squeak. God, Addison makes me so tongue tied. I feel like I always look like such a blustering idiot around her.

Addison's fingers brush against mine on the counter, my breath catching at the sparking feeling.

"Do you want to come sit with us?" She asks, nodding towards her friends.

The machine finally spurts out the last drops of coffee.

"Oh," I fumble with the mug as I pick it up. "Thanks. But I have to get back to work. I was actually getting this for Flora."

The giant tentacled male must overhear me. A loud cracking sound cuts through the room and I turn to see him hitting Sebastian across the back. "Ha! You must be tiring poor Flora out!"

I laugh awkwardly, slipping past Addison and leaving the room. I don't know why I lied about the coffee. I just felt a bit overwhelmed with all her friends in the room and panicked.

Chapter 14

Addison

Well, that was a bust. I flop down onto the couch with a sigh.

Sebastian is choking on his soda after Nereus' comment. It does bring me some joy to see him splutter like that, a deep blush forming around his scales.

"Did you have to scare her off like that?" I ask, flipping my hair and giving Nereus a death glare. He crosses his arms, leaning back in his seat.

I look away and catch eyes with Maddox. He gives me a knowing look, and I can just tell what's coming.

"Why do you care if the human comes or goes?" He huffs.

Fuck. He's caught me there.

"Don't say that you don't." Sebastian chimes in. "We saw you looking at her profile the other day. Come on, tell us what's up."

I run a hand over my face with a groan.

"We kissed."

Maddox gives an excited grunt, "I knew it! You owe me." He holds a hand out to Nereus, one of his tentacles tossing some notes into Maddox's hand.

"Were you guys betting on me? What the fuck?"

I look to Sebastian but he holds his hands up in surrender, chuckling.

"Nothing to do with me."

This is unreal. I can't believe they were betting on me. Actually, I can. This has Nereus written all over it. At least he lost the bet.

"Wait," I look to Maddox. "You were betting that I would kiss her? That's more of an approach I'd expect from Nereus."

"I didn't think you'd have the balls." Nereus cuts across before Maddox can answer.

I open my can of soda, taking a sip and trying to ignore these assholes that I am forced to spend my time with.

"You didn't really tell us what else is going on?" Sebastian brings the topic back to Hyacinth.

"OK," I give in. Better to get this over with. "I have been kind of into her since we met. She is amazing, and I finally had some time alone with her in the studio. One thing led to another and..."

I don't mention that I think we're mates, or that it was Hyacinth's first time with a female. Both of those things just seem too personal to share.

"So what's the problem?" Sebastian asks.

"It's... well, she's never been with a monster before. And I want to give her space to figure things out. But I don't want to give her too much space either."

"Yeah, that makes sense." Sebastian pats my shoulder, squeezing gently.

"Not to me." Nereus cuts across, "She's hot. She has that whole innocent thing going for her. I'm sure a lot of monsters would be into her."

I growl, the vibration working its way up from the depths of me.

"I'm just saying not to give her too much space. Same as you." Nereus puts his hands up in mock surrender.

Maddox glares at Nereus, "I think what he's trying to say is that Hyacinth seems really nice. We think you'd make a great pair, and that you should go for things with her."

Maddox is a sweetheart. Despite being a hulk of a male, standing at nearly seven feet tall, he's a softie. I don't really understand the dynamic between him and Nereus. I don't think they've ever dated, but I could always sniff out their sexual tension from a mile away.

"Yeah," I say, encouraged. "I should at least try to keep things moving with her. Maybe I'll try and spend some time with her tomorrow."

"You've got this." Sebastian's strength is exactly what I need to lean on, sometimes. He really is my best friend.

Chapter 15

Hyacinth

Liliana pulls up in a sleek and expensive looking car. I don't know much about cars, but even I can appreciate the plush interiors as I slide in. I hardly noticed any of this yesterday in my dazed state.

Honestly, I quickly forget about the car again when I see Liliana. She stuns in another one of her sleek suits, this one a black satin. It brings out her darker features, her black horns and the points of her ears.

"Hi there," she purrs, her voice decadent. A chill runs down my spine as she leans over the center console, her fingers brushing against my cheek gently. A pulse of need goes through me, followed by a shiver as she runs one of her black claws gently down my neck.

Liliana reaches further, grabbing the seat belt and buckling me in.

"Thanks," it's the only word I can manage. My mouth is dry and I gulp to help, also to get in some oxygen after that.

She just chuckles, buckling herself in also and switching on the engine.

"I know a small place where you won't be noticed." She tells me. "If you're comfortable with getting dinner on the monster side of town?"

In my nervous state today, I ran through this conversation multiple times. I had realized that Liliana was going to have to take me to dinner in the monster half of the city. So I already know my answer. It's driven mostly by curiosity, as I've never been there before.

"That sounds fun," I tell her. Sinking into my seat a little, I get cozy for the drive.

I try to focus my gaze out of the window as we pull on to the highway, but my eyes keep straying to Liliana. Her clawed hands as they maneuver the stick shift, the way her wings twitch when I can tell that she's annoyed with the other drivers. I wonder what her wings feel like, I didn't get to touch them yesterday. Or her horns, oh how I want to touch her horns.

The outside world finally catches my attention again as we pull off the highway onto a slip road. Tall skyscrapers line the sky in the distance, but we move further away from them. Something catches my peripheral in the sky, and I lean forward to see properly. There are monsters up there, all different shapes flit about, some with wings, some with none. They're too high up to see any detail.

We drive down a main street of a town or suburb, and different Monsters walk the street. It's the evening, so the street is lively. A group of females with translucent wings laugh loudly as they wait to cross the street. They're fairies, if I remember my training properly. A stone skinned gargoyle strolls past them, admiring them as he does.

Holy shit.

It's wild to me that this world has existed right under my nose this whole time. This is fantastic, why are we keeping ourselves from this amazing diversity?

Our car pulls down a derelict looking alleyway and for the first time I wonder if I should have told someone where I was going. Should I be worried? I don't feel worried, I feel completely safe with Liliana.

"This looks sketchy," Liliana chuckles. "I just thought it would be more discreet for us to use the back entrance. And that you might feel more comfortable with it."

"Oh, I don't mind. Thank you for thinking about that." I smile at her, and my usual blush in her presence deepens significantly.

We both get out of the car and enter through a back door, as promised. No one notices us at first, the staff all too busy and preoccupied. Liliana gently grabs the attention of a burly orc male in an apron. He flits away and returns with a male in a polished suit. He would almost look human, if it wasn't for the tiny black horns peaking through his hair.

From what I've learned, he's most likely a demon, like Liliana.

"Liliana," he kisses her on both cheeks in greeting. "This must be Hyacinth."

He gives me a playful wink, but keeps his distance. I smile at him, feeling at ease now that I have gotten a bit more used to the environment.

"Follow me." He grabs two menus and guides us down a hallway. I catch a glimpse of a busy restaurant, but the male leads us further and linto a private room. It's simple, with a table big enough to sit six, but set for two.

The male sets down our menus and leaves us alone.

"This is nice," I say. I look around the room, the dark burgundy and black furnishings are more cozy than creepy. The room is dimly lit by sconces on the walls and candles on the table.

I look down at my outfit, the very out of place patterned jeans and sleeveless shirt.

"You look beautiful. You're cute, and I love how you dress." Liliana says, pulling out my seat for me. "This is one of my favorite restaurants. I remembered they had this private room, so I called ahead earlier to see if it was free."

"That's really considerate, thank you." I try to give her a wholesome smile, but I get distracted. Her blouse dips low as she leans forward to take her seat, her lacy bra peeking out.

"Thirsty?" Liliana asks, snapping me out of my thoughts. I look up to her face and see a knowing smile.

I clear my throat with an awkward giggle. "Yeah, I'm definitely thirsty."

After we order, Liliana gazes at me across the table, leaving a tense silence between us. I try not to squirm in my seat. I don't know how to handle her attention. Before, I was fine if someone flirted with me, I didn't really care. But with Liliana's piercing red eyes staring through me and seeing straight into my soul?

"How was your day?" I manage to ask her. "You were out with a client?"

She tells me about her day and the tension eases some. I can feel myself relaxing more, and I lean forward with my head in my hand as she tells me a story from her day. It's comforting to hear her speak like this.

"So tell me about you." Liliana prompts, as our food arrives and we begin to eat.

"Umm... what do you want to know?" I twirl a fork full of spaghetti and stuff it into my mouth to save me from speaking. It's delicious, and I can't help the little moan of pleasure that I make at the taste.

"Tell me about your family, or your friends."

I tell Liliana about my friends, and how we ended up living together in Riley's house.

"What about your other interests?" I blush under her attention, but I'm feeling more comfortable answering her now.

"Well, I obviously love music. But I also like to game, I play a lot of simple and cozy games. They're really nice to wind down with in the evening or for a relaxing morning."

"Maybe you can show me, I know I could always do with a new hobby." Liliana leans forward in her seat, matching my casual body language with her elbow on the table. It's nice to see her relaxed like this, she's always so put together at work.

"Oh, and I have a pet frog!" I excitedly tell her, sitting up in my seat. "He's thiiiiis big." I hold up my finger and thumb to demonstrate.

"How cute! I've never had a pet before. What's his name?"

Liliana asks me so many questions about Alfred, and it makes me happy to share him with her. I tell her all about getting him and how I look after him. Then I take out my phone and show her photos of him, and show her the tiny mushrooms Samantha made him too.

Normally, people zone out when I tell them about Alfred, but Liliana stays so engaged and it makes me melt a little.

"So tell me about your family." Liliana changes the topic.

"My parents are kind of boring, they live in the countryside." I tell her. "And I have a brother, James. But he's living abroad for college, so I only really see him on the Holidays."

Liliana nods, taking it all in.

"I'm glad you have such close friends then. It's just me and my parents," she tells me. "They live out of town, but I do call them a lot and we're close despite the distance. Oh, and they're mates."

"What do you mean?" I ask, never having heard the term.

Liliana looks shocked, "Mates?"

I shake my head. "I don't know what that means…" I feel a tad awkward as she stares at me dumbfounded.

"Well…" I've never seen Liliana at a loss for words like this.

The demon waiter saves her for a moment as he comes to take our dessert orders. I get my favorite, tiramisu.

Once we're alone again, Liliana finally explains.

"Well, my parents are fated mates. I don't think I've had to explain this before, so I hope I don't mess up. They're meant to be together, not just biologically, but on a soul level too." Liliana looks wistful as she explains it to me, a soft smile on her lips. "Maybe humans call that something different?"

"It sounds beautiful," I tell her. I try not to offend her on a cultural level. It does sound nice, but it's not a concept that I've ever heard of. "I don't think humans have that."

Is it weird that I'm a little disappointed that humans don't have fated mates? It sounds nice, to know that you're perfectly suited to someone.

Liliana explains more over dessert, telling me about omegas and alphas and how all monsters are one or the other. It's fascinating, and I can't help but ask her lots of questions. I may be fascinated, but Liliana is shocked.

"So humans just have *nothing*?!" She exclaims, leaning over the table and grabbing my hand dramatically.

I can't help but giggle at her. Then a thought strikes me.

"Which one are you?" I say it and then I realize it may be offensive.

"Which one do you think I am?" Liliana keeps hold of my hand, heat pulsing through me at her touch. She turns it over, gently dragging her claw along the sensitive skin at my wrist.

"Undoubtedly an alpha." I say, sure of my answer. It has to be that, with how I feel around her. Liliana makes me want to serve her, to worship her.

"Good girl," she purrs.

Holy shit. Pleasure flows through me at her praise.

"And I know that you humans don't think that you have alphas and omegas. But you're definitely an omega, Hyacinth." She leans forward and sniffs the air, which is so much sexier than it sounds. "You have an omega scent, and it's delectable."

Liliana licks her lips for emphasis. I feel like a mouse in a trap when she looks at me like that. A very tiny mouse.

"Would you like to come back to my place, Hyacinth?"

I nod quickly, knowing that I couldn't say no to spending more time with this female.

Chapter 16

Liliana

Hyacinth is devastatingly lovely.

I want to drink in her scent and feel her writhe beneath me. She moaned earlier at dinner and I nearly lost all sense of control right then and there. That little sound will be my undoing.

Oh, and the way she was looking at me, just like she is right now as I drive us to my place.

I could tell that she was self conscious earlier at the restaurant, and I feel bad for not giving her enough of a heads up about the dinner beforehand. It took me long enough to get the guts to send her the text in the first place, though. After my conversation with my parents yesterday, I knew I needed to make a concerted effort with my little human.

We don't speak much again while I drive. But I kind of like it this way. Hyacinth is fascinated by what she can see outside, and I get to enjoy the look of wonder on her face.

I pull us into my building and park up the car. Getting out quickly to grab the door for Hyacinth before she can get to it herself. She deserves to be treated like the princess she is. Holding out my hand to her, I don't let go as I close the door behind her and walk us up to my penthouse.

"We can finally have some wine now," I say as I let us in the door, placing my car keys on the side table.

Hyacinth wanders in slowly behind me, taking the space in with her meticulous gaze.

"Why don't you go get comfortable on the couch?" I suggest, gesturing in that direction. I head into the kitchen and pour the wine.

Something primal awakens in me with the knowledge that my mate is in my home. It's satisfying, but still leaves me wanting more. I know how I want this evening to end.

Carrying both glasses back into the living space, I slip off my shoes carefully before moving to join Hyacinth. She's switched on a lamp, and the soft light makes her brown skin glow. My eyes trace her wrist right up to her shoulder, as she takes the glass from me. I like her in these sleeveless tops, her full arms on display. Her skin looks so soft, but I hold myself back from touching her right away.

I cozy up next to her on the couch, my feet folded neatly beneath me as I drape my arm across the back of the seat.

"Thank you for dinner." Hyacinth leans closer to me. Her shoulder brushing against my arm, her thigh pressing against my knee. I want to let her lean into me completely.

We need to talk first, though.

"You're welcome, princess." I give her what I hope is a cheeky grin. Winding one of her curls around my finger, I press on. "I wanted to speak with you about yesterday, but I didn't think that the restaurant was an appropriate place to do that."

Hyacinth lets out a sigh, before nodding to herself.

"So... I kissed another female yesterday. *Before* I ran into you in the hallway." She waits to gauge my reaction.

"I'm not surprised." I tell her. "I assumed something must have happened to set you off."

I continue gently playing with her hair as she continues. "Oh. Well, yeah. So, I kissed someone, and it was great. But then I panicked and ran away and I saw you. But I had never kissed a girl before and I just... I was surprised with myself.

"And this whole time..." She looks up at me, her little hand coming to rest on me. "This whole time I was attracted to you. I just thought it was because you were a succubus. I'm sorry that it took me kissing someone else to realize that I liked you for real."

Hyacinth glances down, not quite able to meet my eyes now.

"Oh, baby." I set my wine glass down and do the same with hers. I pull her to me and she snuggles closer, resting her head on my arm and looking up at me with those chocolate brown orbs.

Whoever this other female she kissed is could be our third. A nervous energy fills me just thinking about it.

"How are you feeling now?" I ask. "Would you like to continue exploring things with me?"

"I would like to try kissing you again," she says.

Perfectly pouted, pink lips turn towards me and I gently cup Hyacinth's face. My lips brush hers, ever so slightly, and I lean back to see how she reacts.

She eagerly follows me, crushing her lips to mine. I sink into the blissful feeling of holding my beautiful human in my arms. She fits snuggly against me as she climbs into my lap.

After my shock wears off at her forwardness, my hands start to roam her delicate body. She feels divine, her fingernails scraping against my scalp as she grips my hair.

We tangle tongues, my pussy growing quickly damp as she presses herself even closer to me.

Chapter 17

Hyacinth

I can't get enough of Liliana. I grind myself against her hard stomach as I try to deepen our kiss even further.

Normally, I'm much more of a passenger in these types of situations. But I can't help but take what I want. Liliana is divine. Our tongues move against each other and I notice that it doesn't feel normal in shape. Is her tongue shifting?

Gasping, I pull away. "What..?"

"You're not with a human now, Hyacinth." Liliana chuckles as she tidies my hair away from my face. "Let me take you to my bedroom? I will show you what it's like to fuck a succubus..."

I find myself nodding with comical speed as she scoops me up into her arms. My arms snake around her neck. I don't think anyone has ever carried me like this before.

Liliana takes us into her bedroom. It's as plush and expensive looking as the rest of her apartment. A fluffy rug covers the majority of the floor, and my toes sink into it as she sets me down. She bends over so that her red eyes can meet mine.

"Do you have any limits, Hyacinth? Anything you don't want me to do?"

Do I? "I-I don't know." I answer honestly. I have no idea what she is even capable of, as a succubus. But beyond that... sex has always been very basic for me.

"We should come up with a system then. OK?" I've never seen Liliana look as tender as she does in this moment. Her lack of that usual, hardened exterior makes me feel vulnerable in a way that I wasn't expecting.

"If you immediately don't like something I am doing, you'll say red." She cups my face gently, "If you're unsure or you want me to slow down, you'll say orange."

Liliana starts to unbutton my blouse as she speaks. I feel helpless, my arms hanging by my sides, unsure of what to do.

"If I check in and you like what's happening, you'll say green." She slips my blouse off over my arms, exposing my stomach and boobs to her. Her gaze goes hungry as she looks down at me, her fangs showing when she opens her mouth to speak again. "You got that, princess?"

"Y-yes," I whimper. It seems simple enough, though I'm not sure that there is anything she could do to me that I wouldn't want.

"Good pet," she leans forward to taste my neck, slowly running her tongue down to my collar bone and sending a shiver through my spine. "Do I have your permission to use my powers on you?"

"Yes." I say, more assuredly this time. My hands push at her clothes, clumsily trying to take them off. Liliana sinks onto her knees in front of me, sliding my jeans down and giving me the most wicked grin.

Liliana's touches change. While they gave me pleasure before, a needy desire floods through me at every point of contact. My hands tangle in her hair for balance, the thick, glossy strands like silk in my hands. The deep red of her hair looks even richer against the creamy backdrop of her bedroom.

"You can touch my horns, you know." Liliana suggests, trailing kisses down my stomach.

I had been afraid of where I should or shouldn't touch. What if it had been some great offense to touch her horns or her wings. I gently grasp the straight black horns, they are sleek and polished, almost slippery.

"Can I touch your wings?" I ask, tentatively eyeing the red and black membranes.

Liliana finally frees me of my jeans before answering.

"You can touch me *everywhere*, princess."

Instead of actually letting me touch her wings, she stands and swiftly picks me up again. Instinctively, I wrap my legs around her waist. I can see her eyes widen when she feels my soaking panties pressed up against her.

I've never been this wet before. Even that thought has me growing even wetter again. The feel of our bodies pressed up against each other is almost too intense, now that she is fully using her abilities. My nipples are peaked, pressing hard against my bra.

Liliana gently sits me on the edge of the bed, pulling back to look at me. I don't feel as self conscious as I expected, or at least not until it dawns on me that she is still fully clothed.

"Strip for me," I don't recognize the sultry sound of my own voice. I think something in Liliana's powers helped to strip away some of my normal inhibitions. It's so freeing. I could get drunk on this feeling.

I lean back on my elbows, my boobs pushed up into the air as I watch. Liliana takes off her blazer first, the piece thrown to the side as she unbuttons her pants. I bite my lip as I eagerly wait, my pussy clenching as she undoes the bow on her blouse. The action reveals a sliver of a glimpse of her cleavage. She pulls the top over her head, showing me her glistening porcelain torso. She is all hard, toned muscle.

Instead of removing her pants, Liliana reaches into the pocket, pulling out a hair tie. Her toned arms flex as she ties her hair back into a ponytail. I didn't think that action could be so sexy, her boobs pushed out and jiggling as she moves. Her pants come off quickly now as she gets on to her knees before me again, and I lose my chance to see much of her lower half.

Our heads are level with one another in this position. I like Liliana's hair pulled back, her prominent cheekbones even more defined. Her pointed ears are on full show as I reach out to touch the black tip of one. Liliana moans beneath my touch, her hips jerking.

"Are your ears sensitive?" I tease, continuing to stroke it.

"My ears, my horns, my wings..." She lists, reminding me again of the giant sprawl of wings behind her. She flexes them, so that they reach around to touch the bed on either side of me.

My legs press against her hips as I lean forward, stretching out my arm. Her wings are stiffer than I imagined, with how delicate they look. I suppose they have to be stiff to carry her weight when she flies. I turn to ask her, but I am distracted by the needy whimper that Liliana lets out.

I'm pulled away from her wing and into her arms, her lips pressing hungrily against mine. I'm the one whimpering now, as hot tremors of need pound through my pussy. I lose myself in our kiss, my body becoming a pliable, needy mess.

Liliana shifts, kissing down my neck and reaching behind me to unclasp my bra. Once she's ridden me of it, her hands move to cup my boobs. She flicks out her tongue, quickly flicking against my nipple and I cry out with the pleasure.

"You make the best noises for me, little pet."

I let out a whine at her words, and that seems to spur her into action. She tears my underwear off, the loud rip cutting through the room. Liliana kisses up my inner thigh, and I realize what she's about to do.

"Wait." I say, panting heavily. She stills against me while I try to make my words come out. "I... I-I've never had... Nobody's ever..."

Liliana looks up at me intently. "Are you a virgin, little pet?"

"No!" I exclaim. "I just…"

"Oh," a dark, almost possessive gleam enters her eyes. "Has no one ever gone down on you before?"

I shake my head quickly, squirming with my embarrassment.

"Human men sound like idiots." Liliana says simply, before going back to kissing my thigh.

"Remember your words, and use them if you need." She mumbles against me, her kisses growing closer to my aching and exposed pussy.

She drapes my leg over her shoulder, scooting my ass closer to the edge of the bed. I fall back onto the sheets from the movement. My toes brush against her wing, and I drag my foot up and down against one, earning myself a deep throaty moan from Liliana.

Her claws tickle as she teases the outside of my pussy, before she uses the pads of her fingers to spread me open. The cold air shocks me before her hot breath covers me. Her wet tongue slides across my clit. A spark of pleasure shoots straight through me, lighting all of my nerve endings on fire. I had no idea this would feel like this.

"You taste so *good*." She moans against me, her tongue exploring me further. Liliana lifts my other leg over her shoulder, burying her face in me completely.

I fist the sheets tightly as her tongue delves into my pussy.

"Oh, *fuck*." I cry out as her tongue shifts again, like it did when we were kissing earlier. Only this time it thickens and lengthens, filling me completely.

A weird sensation fills me, and it takes me a moment to register that her tongue is *vibrating*. I writhe against her, my hands moving to cup my boobs as a pressure builds. Liliana presses against a point inside me that has my eyes rolling back with pleasure. I lose myself completely in the sensations, my body moving of its own accord.

The vibrations grow in intensity, and I try to pull away, the feeling becoming too intense. Liliana grips my hips, holding me in place. Her fingers gently stroke against me, almost telling me to relax. I try, taking a deep breath and ease back into the feeling.

The pressure builds again, much quicker this time. I relax into it now, and I couldn't pull away if I tried. I let myself go as it increases into a wave of pleasure that crashes through my body.

Trembling, I reach down to grip Liliana's horns, pulling her up to me. I've never felt this way before. It feels so vulnerable and I just want to be held by her.

Liliana braces herself over me, her fangs showing as she smiles at me. Her mouth and chin are covered in my wetness, her wings loom over us both, caging us in. She licks her lips as she looks down at me. I jolt as something wraps around my ankle, my body still so sensitive. I try to look down before realizing that it must be her tail. I had forgotten about it in the heat of the moment.

"Can we snuggle for a minute?" I ask.

Her face softens immediately, "Of course, baby."

I'm scooped up into her arms and before I know it I am draped across her chest as she lounges on the bed. I'm practically laying on top of her, as her wings span out beneath us. Her tail is still wound around my ankle, and I realize that I like it there. It's comforting to be tied to her in some way.

I press my head into her soft boobs and sigh contentedly. I still feel so good, and tremors rack through me occasionally.

That was amazing.

That was also my first orgasm. I chuckle into her chest as the realization hits.

"What is it?" she asks, her voice lined with mischief.

"I... that was my first orgasm." I decide to just go for it and tell her.

"Human men are definitely stupid." That's all she says on the matter. And I like that she makes it more about them than she does about me.

"Well, they don't have shifting, vibrating tongues." I tease, moving to straddle her and sitting up. I look her over, "And they're not nearly as sexy as you."

Her bra has a clasp in the front, and I undo it, letting the material fall away. Again, her boobs are so different from mine, just like the rest of her. Her nipples are black buds against her white skin. I press the flat of my tongue against one, slowly dragging it across. I can feel Liliana shiver beneath me. It makes me feel powerful that I can make this stunning succubus shiver.

"Mhmm... good pet..." she groans as I move to her other nipple. I tease them both with my tongue, before sucking on one as I gently pinch the other. What surprises me is the pleasure I feel as I tend to her. My pussy grows damp again and I know she can feel it slipping against her stomach.

Liliana grips my ass cheeks, pressing my pussy forward to grind against her. I want this to be about her though. I want to give my monster her pleasure.

I move down so I am nestled between her legs. Her delicate lace panties leave nothing to the imagination. Reaching down, I gently run a finger over the fabric covering her mound and it comes away soaking. She is so wet for me.

That almost seems past my comprehension levels at the moment.

Lifting the waistband of her panties to pull them down, I'm surprised when she reaches out a claw and slices right through them. She grips my hair tightly and pushes my head down between her legs.

I'm faced with her glistening pussy, and my brain short circuits. What do I do? I tentatively flick my tongue over the hood of her clit. We both moan at the same time. She tastes amazing. I go back in, more assuredly this time, circling her clit.

I slip a finger into her and curl upwards, trying to hit that same spot for her.

"Two," she moans, grinding against me. I add a second finger, all while keeping my pace, circling her clit with my tongue. It isn't long before her legs are tightening around me, her pussy quivering as she cums on my fingers.

I don't want to stop, working her through it and into another orgasm.

"OK pet," she sighs, pulling my head away from her. I understand her self-satisfied look from earlier now. Seeing her undone beneath me like this is such a privilege.

Parts of her hair have come loose, her chest heaving, her wings splayed out.

"You're a Goddess." I tell her. She looks otherworldly, so stunning. I can't believe that I still have my fingers inside this beauty.

Chapter 18

Hyacinth

The heady aroma of coffee wakes me, along with the early glow of morning filling the room. My mind starts to wander to last night, and I can feel the blush forming on my face. It was incredible, I've never felt any kind of pleasure like that before.

A stunning and very naked succubus strolls into the room. I can feel my pussy dampening at the sight of her form almost immediately.

"Good morning, princess." She says, handing me a cup of coffee. I sit up a bit as she scoots back into the bed.

Liliana takes a few seconds to fluff up our pillows before snuggling up next to me.

"Morning," I lean forward and kiss her lips, basking in the feeling.

She was so good last night after we had sex, and we had cleaned up and got into bed again. I spent the night cuddled into her side, her wings wrapped protectively around me. I don't think I've ever slept better than that.

I take a sip of my coffee, made with cinnamon and honey, just how I like. Smiling over the rim at her, I get lost in her beautiful gaze.

"Did you have a good time last night?" Liliana asks, running her claws down my arm.

"Of course I did." I giggle at myself, fully aware that I answered too quickly. I add, a little hesitantly, "did you?"

"Oh, I had a fantastic time, little pet." The sultry promise in her voice makes my toes curl. Her tail strokes my leg in a comforting motion. I take another sip of my coffee and shift closer to her.

I let out a sigh, pure contentment pouring through me.

I can't believe that she enjoyed herself, that she might want to do this again. I could get used to this, sexy nights and cozy mornings with my succubus. But my thoughts stray to a certain purple haired witch. Last night was amazing, but I wouldn't want to lose out on spending more time with Addison. Did I rush into things with Liliana?

"I was thinking about the person you kissed." Liliana speaks, shocking me with how in sync her thoughts are with mine. "I don't want you to feel like you need to stop seeing them."

I nearly choke on my coffee. "Really?" I stumble over my words, nearly spilling the entire cup over her pristine sheets.

"This is all new to you, being with a female... I want you to be able to feel like you can explore whatever you need to with that other person."

Liliana takes our coffees, setting them on the night stand. She pulls me into her arms properly, her hand stroking my cheek.

"Just so I am being clear. I want you, Hyacinth. I don't think I can let you go after last night. But I also don't want you to feel trapped in that. You're young, you're just coming into yourself, realizing your tastes... all I ask is that we keep an open communication around it all."

"Oh," I reply. "If you're sure."

Liliana kisses my neck, nodding against my skin there and tickling me.

"I just want you to be satisfied, princess." She continues to kiss down my neck and takes her time getting to my nipple. I'm aching once she gets there.

"Do you remember your words I taught you. The colors?"

"Yes," I whimper as she gently grazes my boob with a fang. Would she bite me with them?

"Good pet." I feel her tail unwinding from around my leg, slowly moving higher, tickling me as it moves. It runs the full length of my torso, the tip resting in the air above my face. "Open up and get this tail nice and wet for me, pet."

I open my mouth and she fucks it with her tail. I suck on it and coat it as best as I can.

"That's it," she pulls her tail away from me, "such a good little pet." I whine as she uses her leg to spread mine, her tail delving closer to my pussy.

"Are you going to…?" I realize her intent as she presses her tail inside me slowly. The tapered tip stretching me wide before the head disappears inside me entirely.

Liliana pulls me onto her lap, kissing me deeply as her tail starts to move inside me. I grind against her, the friction sending me to new heights as we kiss. I want her to feel good too, so I reach up and play with the tip of her ear, my other hand stroking her wing.

We writhe against one another, caught up in our plea-sure. Liliana shifts her tongue in my mouth, fucking me there too as her tail pounds into me now.

I come undone quickly, my hands gripping her horns tight as she follows me. It's a different sort of orgasm this time, almost refreshing in my morning haze.

Relaxing my hold on her horns, I bury my face in her chest as her tail eases out of me. Oh shit, I can feel my cum leak out of me with it.

"I think we need a shower," I giggle.

The ride to the studio was perfect. Liliana made us fresh coffees and put them in flasks for us. She even packed me a pastry for the ride.

She had also given me some much needed fresh under-wear. My clothes had come off quickly the night before, so I just wore them again.

"I'll get you some things to keep here," she had told me, her hand in mine as we had walked down to the car.

She gave me a discreet kiss on the cheek when she pulled up to the Studio. Dropping me off, she headed back to her client again today.

I hated watching her leave, wishing we could go back to bed together for the day.

Walking into the studio, I see Flora and Alex are there already.

"Hey guys," I say. Starting to get set up, moving my things into place.

"Where were you last night?" Alex asks, a jokingly suspicious edge to their voice.

"W-what? Why would you ask that?" I stumble, surprised. What had they seen?

"Those are the same clothes you wore yesterday..." Alex teases.

"Leave her alone," Flora chimes in. "Let's get to work."

I almost got caught with that one. Time to start keeping some overnight things with me.

My phone buzzes, and I see I have a text from Addison, asking me to get lunch with her today.

"Look at her grin," Alex taunts, "she's definitely seeing someone."

I jokingly slap them on the back, laughing it off. My joy at getting to see Addison today outweighs their teasing.

Chapter 19

Hyacinth

We keep working until lunch time, and I quickly pack up my bag when Flora says that we should break to eat.

"Where are you going?" Alex asks. "Do you not want to eat with us?"

"Umm.. I'm meeting someone for lunch." I can feel the blush spread across my cheeks and even Flora looks interested this time.

"Who are you meeting?" Flora asks, a suggestive hitch in her voice. She flicks her golden hair over a shoulder as she waits.

"Fine, OK." I know giving in is the easiest and quickest way to leave. "I'm meeting Addison for lunch, if you must know."

"Sebastian's Addison?"

"Can we come?"

Flora and Alex both speak at the same time.

"Yes, Flora, Addison who works with Sebastian." There is a part of me that hates how she phrased that. She's not *Sebastian's* Addison. "And no, I'd prefer if you didn't come... it's kind of a date."

"*Hyacinth*!" Flora squeals, grabbing onto my arms. "That's so exciting! Go, go, take the afternoon off to spend it with Addison."

She turns to Alex, gushing at them and I take the opportunity to slip out the door.

I groan, maybe it was a mistake to share that with them. But I could tell that they weren't going to give up on it. Oh, I hope this lunch goes well, otherwise I'm going to have to deal with telling the pair that it didn't work out. I wonder what they would think about me dating Liliana?

Checking my phone, I see a text from Addison to meet her out front.

She's wearing a really pretty blue sundress, the hem reaching her knees and leaving a lot of her creamy skin on display. Her violet eyes offset stunningly against the color, especially when they light up in recognition.

"Hyacinth!" She walks up to me, bending down to kiss me on the cheek before taking my hand in hers.

"Hi Addison," I am back to being a nervous mess. All of the sexual prowess that I had last night has left me. "You look really pretty in that dress."

Her smile lights up at my compliment, "I was thinking I might take you on a picnic. Would you like that?"

"Sounds great!" I squeeze her hand in mine. "Also, I have the afternoon off. I don't know if you need to get back to work but..."

"Oh, that's great! I wasn't even working today." She tugs me along, "Come on, I'll drive us there."

She came to the studio on her day off to come and meet me? That is so sweet. Plus, it sounds like she made a picnic too.

When we get to her car, I'm surprised by how normal it is. Addison is kind of small for a monster, now that I think about it. She's still much taller than me, but more like a tall human woman. In fact, if you could explain away her eye color as contacts and her hair as dyed, she could maybe pass for a human.

"Do you ever sneak into the human side of the city?" I blurt.

Addison devolves into fits of tinkling laughter, and I wait patiently outside her car. I'm not sure why she's laughing, but it's contagious enough to put a smile on my face.

"I'm sorry," she heaves. "Get in the car and I will tell you all about it."

We cozy up in the vehicle, getting settled, while Addison tells me her story.

"I'm guessing that you're assuming that I can pass as a human. Which, in short, I can."

Addison pulls out of the parking lot and heads towards Center Park.

"Once I was old enough to drive, I used to sneak out to the human side of the city. It was innocent enough, I would go shopping there so I could have clothes no one else did at school. That kind of thing.

"It's when I got old enough to drink that I had a bit of trouble. I thought I would be fine if anything were to go wrong. I was the monster, you know? But I had a run in with some human men at one point that wasn't great."

She reaches across the car to squeeze my leg. "Not something that I want to get into right now, though."

"Yeah, of course!" I chime, trying to lighten the mood.

I am angry though. I feel a bit responsible that something happened to poor Addison while in the human side of town. I know that it's irrational, and I had nothing to do with it. But it unsettles me. I didn't even think about monsters blending in with us. I wonder what other horrible things have happened?

The ride to the park doesn't take long, it's actually pretty close to the studio. I should come here more often, I realize. It's really pretty in the sun. There are long lawns, dotted with picnic benches, all bordered by a canopy of trees and patches of wildflowers.

"This is lovely," I comment, getting out of the car.

Addison pops the trunk and I help her with what she has in there. It's a lot. She really thought this through and prepared. My heart melts at the thought.

I take the blanket and she grabs the giant basket and we take a stroll to find the right spot.

"We're going to need to pick a spot in the shade," she says, gesturing to her creamy skin. Oh, I hadn't even thought about that. I'm sure she burns up to a crisp.

"Do you have sunscreen?"

After I've made sure that she has taken the necessary precautions, we pick a cute spot next to the edge of the green space. The table is almost nestled in a patch of purple wildflowers that match Addison's hair perfectly.

I roll out the blanket to work as a sort of tablecloth and Addison starts to set up her spread.

"I know you like to bring in your cute packed lunches," Addison starts. She noticed that? "So I thought a picnic might be the best way to elevate that. I'm not a cook, but I *can* assemble some good ingredients."

This is all so sweet, I almost can't handle it. Addison pulls out a variety of different bits and pieces. Olives, crackers, meats, cheeses, fruits... It's a full assortment. I feel spoiled right now, and I kind of love it.

"Wow, this all looks so good."

Addison turns to face me, playfully popping a grape into her mouth. She dangles a second out to me, holding it up close to my face. I open my lips to let her feed me, my tongue grazing against her finger a little. The interaction sends a shiver straight to my pussy.

Her violet eyes light up, and I know she has accomplished what she wanted.

We sit next to each other on the bench, the food splayed out before us. Addison presses closer to me with a flirty smile.

"How are you doing?" She asks, starting to pick at the food.

"I'm good. And I'm sorry I was kind of awkward in the break room yesterday. I think I was just feeling a bit weird around your friends." I try to busy myself with spreading cheese on a cracker. "They're kind of intimidating for me."

"Oh, Hyacinth." She sighs, but it's lighthearted. "They're all softies really. Well, except Nereus, to be honest I don't know what he is."

I giggle at her joke.

"No, I know. I was just being a bit weird in the moment."

She presses up closer to me, turning so her face is inches from mine. "Do I make you nervous, little one?"

My hand moves to her leg of its own accord, my thoughts focused on Addison's bright eyes, her plush lips.

I nod, ever so slightly. "But I like it."

Addison leans close enough that I can feel the ghost of her lips against mine. Growing impatient, I press forward, a little sigh escaping me. God, it feels so good to be kissing her again.

She pulls away though, "I figure I should save you for dessert."

I can't help the fit of giggles that escapes me. We work our way through the food as we chat.

"You have *six* sisters?" I am shocked. That is a crazy number. "Your house must have been wild growing up!"

"It's a witch thing," Addison sighs. "I don't dislike them individually. But altogether it's too much for me. I was there this past Sunday, and it was so draining. Moving out on my own was the best thing I have done for myself."

"What do you mean it's a witch thing?" I cover my mouth, chewing on some salami.

"We strengthen our powers as a family. It's a ritual we do. So the more family we have, the stronger we are as a whole."

I find myself intrigued, and I realize that I really don't know much about witches. I really don't know anything about what kind of powers Addison may have.

"What does it mean to be a witch then? What do your powers do?"

She pecks me on the cheek before moving to stand up. Holding out her hands in front of her, Addison creates a crackle of energy. It looks like lightning, but on a much smaller scale, in a striking violet color. Her eyes glow, more so than usual, her hair floats out and around her head. It's beautiful.

"I can manipulate electricity," she says, settling back down next to me. "My family are electro witches, but there are other kinds of witches as well. I can manipulate technology too, although that takes a lot more skill than natural ability."

"So you do use magic to make music!" I exclaim.

She just chuckles at me, "Change of subject, little one. But I wanted to ask you something."

"Sure! I'm an open book." I fold my leg up under me as I watch Addison nibble on her lip.

"I saw... on your socials, I saw you with a guy. He's not your boyfriend, is he?"

I quickly comb through my thoughts as I shake my head, trying to think of who she might be talking about.

"No, I don't have a boyfriend... what photo made you think that?"

She pulls out her phone, showing me some snaps from the brunch at the weekend.

"Oh... Chris is definitely not my boyfriend!" I visibly shiver at the thought. "I'm pretty sure that I'm not into guys at all."

"It's OK if you were, I was just curious is all." She rests her hand on my leg, leaning forward to brush her lips against my ear. "I also wanted to make sure it was OK to spend the rest of the day with you..."

My neck tingles with the suggestive tone in her voice, my toes curling.

"Did you want to come back to my place?" I bravely suggest. "There shouldn't be anyone else home. So we'd have the place to ourselves..."

Chapter 20

*A*ddison

Thankfully, the drive to Hyacinth's home isn't far. I have to concentrate hard to get us there safely, her fresh and citrusy scent a distraction. Not to mention the way she bites on her lip when she is thinking.

"How come you had the day off today?" She asks me.

"Oh, well, I was at an awards show last night."

I pull the car in, as the map says we are at the destination. Hyacinth unbuckles her belt, so we must be at the right place.

"Ooh! How exciting!" Hyacinth starts the walk up the drive of a pretty, detached home. I take a look around, glancing at the picturesque suburban atmosphere. I'm glad to see that she's living somewhere safe.

"Were you up for an award?" She continues speaking, unlocking the door to a tidy but lived in home.

"Yeah..." I am not sure how much to tell her, not wanting to come off as bragging. Her chocolatey doe eyes look up at me expectantly, and I have no choice but to indulge her. "Well, Sebastian's newest album was up for an award. And we collab on everything, so we both accepted it."

"Wait, so you won?!" She squeals, pulling me in for a tight hug. "Why didn't you say anything?"

A joy I haven't felt in a long time overwhelms me. Warmth spreads across my chest as I hug her back, feeling our connection and how happy she is for me. I wrap my arms around her tiny form, holding her close to my chest.

"It's not exactly something you lead with..." I joke. "But yeah, OK. I will brag for a second. Seb and I won album of the year for the fourth time."

Hyacinth keeps her arms wrapped tight around me, but she leans back to look me in the eye. "That is so fucking cool, Addison."

"Come on," She continues with a giggle. "Let's get out of my hallway."

We grab some sodas from her well stocked fridge. She explains that her friend, Riley, buys and makes all her food. I'm proud of the life my little human has made for herself, she seems well cared for and on a great path.

"Wanna hang out in my room?" There's a nervous energy about her when she asks, picking at the label on her soda.

"Definitely."

Her room is adorable, and so perfectly Hyacinth. There are shelves packed full with all her collections, a cute bed covered in throw blankets and plushies, and a pretty intense mixing set up for a graduate. Her desk has a solid mixing desk, other sound equipment, and a glass ball filled with plants. That part doesn't fit.

I move over to it, seeing a pretty yellow orchid inside.

"That's Alfred!" She excitedly tells me, gesturing at the orb.

"What's Alfred?" I ask, leaning closer to see what she means. Is there an animal in there?

"Not what... who! Alfred's my pet frog... look he's under there." Oh, that makes more sense. Why is her excited face as she points out her pet to me the cutest thing I've ever seen?

I eventually spot the tiny guy hiding under a leaf, it's yellow and brown body obvious now that I know where he is.

"Awh, he's cute." I tell her, pulling her to me so I can tuck her head under my chin while I watch her frog with her.

"Wanna play a video game?" She asks, picking up a controller and offering it to me. Like everything else in her room, it matches the mushroom forest theme, with cute stickers all over it.

We get cozy on Hyacinth's bed as she talks me through how to play the game and use her controller. I'm pretty decent at gaming, and it seems simple enough.

Grabbing a squishy plushie that's an adorable green frog, I set it on my lap to rest my wrists on. Hyacinth leans up against me, her flyaway curls tickling my arm as she settles in.

We play for a bit, it's essentially a game where our players have to collect floating diamonds and stars for boosts. It's nice and easy, but we still laugh when either of us make a mistake. The tricky part is when the levels start to speed up, that's when I can feel she is going to win.

Unfortunately for Hyacinth, I can't allow that. I guide a gentle shock of electricity to her wrist. Her fingers fumble on the buttons as planned and I squeal as her player falls off the ledge, signaling me as the winner.

"Addison!" She snatches my controller from my hand, sliding onto my lap as she laughs. "Don't think I didn't notice that!"

"I don't know what you're talking about..." I grip her hips, flipping us so that she is laying underneath me, her legs still wrapped around my waist. Her giggles die down and turn into a low moan. "I am ready to claim my prize, though."

I lean forward, hearing her breath quicken as I do. Her skin glows in the low lights of the LED strips around her room. Her small hands come to my nape, gently gripping my hair there.

"Then claim it." She whispers.

I don't need any more encouragement than that. My kiss isn't gentle, I ravish her. Back arching, I press my core against hers and we moan together. The tantalizing sound she makes gets lost in our kisses. Running my hands up her waist, I start to slip her blouse up higher. I leave a crackle of energy in the wake of my hands, causing her to shiver.

"Are you home, Hyacinth?" A man speaks loudly, busting into the room without a care in the world. I have to hold in a snarl as I push Hyacinth behind me, covering her with my body.

"Get out!" She screeches, tossing the frog plushie at him.

He catches it easily, moving further into the room.

"Who do we have here?" He wiggles his brows at me.

Oh, this must be Riley. My nerves get the better of me, wondering what his reaction to a surprise monster in his house will be. I think back to those human men... No. Riley looks after Hyacinth. He's not like them, he's a good man. Riley looks gentle, with a kind and soft featured face, his hair a striking shade of copper.

"So this is where you were last night?" He asks Hyacinth when neither of us speak.

Where she was last night?

"I'm Riley." He holds his hand out to me in a kind gesture. I take it, but quickly turn when I notice that Hyacinth's breath has quickened.

"Please, can you leave Riley?" She tries to seem calm, but I notice the tiny hitch in her breath, the rise and fall of her chest speeding up. "I need to speak with Addison about something."

I don't look back at him, but I can hear the door click shut.

"Addison, I'm so sorry." She pulls away from me, tucking her knees up and under her chin.

"Shh... come here." I pull her back into a hug. Nuzzling at her neck, she moves her head to bare it to me in submission. Taking in a long inhale, I scent it.

I can smell the lingering scent of an alpha on her, a hint of a red berry. Which is weird because I don't normally smell things like that on people. But I also don't really get this close to anyone these days anyway.

I wonder who else she has been spending time with? It's only been a couple days since we kissed, so she's certainly been busy. I have to admit that I like the smell on her, and that's new for me too. It's not that I'm normally the jealous type, but I didn't think I would be into smelling someone else on my little human.

This is obviously what Riley was referring to, and why my little Hyacinth is freaking out right now. She feels caught out. But I told her that she could explore things with other people.

I run my hands down her back, gently soothing her.

"Talk to me," I pull away a little to see her face. The wrongness in seeing her tear stained cheeks cuts me to my core. My poor little human.

"I'm sorry," she sniffles again. "I should have talked to you about this before we kissed again. But I'm stupid and I got caught up in the moment, and you're just so pretty and I—"

"Hey," I continue stroking her, showing her with my touch that I'm OK. "Please, it's OK. Would it have been nice if Riley hadn't been the one to tell me? Sure. But I meant it when I said that you can see other people, Hyacinth. I don't think you're going to scare me off at this point."

She seems to steel herself for a moment before opening up to me.

"I slept with someone last night. A female someone."

"An alpha?" I guess, wiping her tears from her face now that she's calmed down a bit.

"How did you know?" She asks, confirming my suspicions.

"I can smell them on you, I think. Just a lingering scent."

"God," she exclaims. "I am in such a weird position right now. I haven't been interested in anyone in years, or ever really. And now all of a sudden I'm attracted to two of you!"

Hyacinth is so young, and I do forget that at times. It was only a week ago that I had looked down on the idea of a graduate going to coffee with me, thinking that they would be too young to keep up with the conversation.

She is growing into herself, and I don't want to be the one to push her. My gut is telling me that Hyacinth is mine. But I can wait, I can give her the space that she needs.

"It's completely normal for you to like two people at once, you know." Her warm body is still pressed up against mine, so I slip back against the pillows to make us more comfortable. "From what I've observed, you humans are really hung up on the whole monogamy thing. But with monsters, it's different. Once we've found our mate or mates, we tend not to see other people, but I think that's just because they don't measure up. But if you haven't found your mates? It's much more fluid and free."

"So this is normal?" Her brown orbs look at me without any shield, her vulnerability humbles me.

"Perfectly normal," I assure her. "You can take all the time and space you need."

I want to tell her that I know she's mine. But I also don't want to undermine anything I have just said.

Hyacinth rests her head on my chest. I can feel her breath calming as she snuggles in. It feels perfect, her legs tangled with mine and my arms wrapped around her.

After a while, I suggest we play some more games, promising not to cheat this time.

Chapter 21

Hyacinth

I feel like a tool.

Addison deserves better than this, with the pretty date that she planned for us. It should have been me that she heard this all from.

Riley was obviously just having a bit of fun, but I'm still feeling frustration towards him right now.

I can't help my giggle as I look over at her, the console gripped tightly in her hands. She bites her lip as she concentrates, the levels in our game getting harder. Addison can try all she wants, but she's not winning this round.

Not that she won the last round either, the sneaky cheat. I jolt a bit at the memory of the shock she sent to my wrist. My pussy had clenched at the sensation, which was even more of a surprise than the shock itself.

None of my previous sexual experiences were very adventurous, prior to last night of course. So I don't really know all the possibilities of what I like or don't like. But I definitely never thought I would get a sexual response from an electric shock.

The wetness pooling in my panties says otherwise. The thought of Addison using her powers in other places on my body...

I pause our game, my gaze traveling up the smooth legs stretched out before Addison. My hands are there before I even realize, sliding up and under her dress to rest on her thigh. The supple feel of her beneath my touch feels amazing.

Addison gently tugs my face towards hers, pulling me into a decadent kiss. We take our time with one another, moving at a languid pace. My hands curl into her silky soft hair, and I sigh into her mouth.

She takes the opportunity to tangle her tongue with mine, and a different type of lightning fills my veins. Her hands explore my body in gentle caresses until they come to rest on my boobs, massaging me there through my clothes.

"Let's take this off. Shall we?" She asks, pulling away from me as she begins to unbutton my blouse. All I can do is sigh and moan, nodding my head in consent.

Once my blouse is shed, Addison leans back to look at me. I glance down at my boobs cupped in the lacy bra, the balconette shape leaving a lot of skin on display.

"You're so fucking sexy, Hyacinth." She pulls the soft cup of my bra down and frees one boob. Her tongue slips out, teasing at my nipple and I grind against nothing at the pleasure.

"Here." Addison tugs me onto her so that I am straddling her leg, I grind against her as she teases my nipples. It's a good thing I'm still wearing my jeans, because I feel so slick I know I would be staining her dress otherwise.

I lean back a moment and push her dress up around her hips. A scrap of damp lace is covering her pussy. Have I done this to her? Brushing my fingers against it, it's even wetter than I had thought. I shove her panties aside so I can rub against her wetness.

Addison's head tips back as I gently rub up against her clit.

"Lay back," I tell her. I move in between her legs, still rubbing her clit as I do so. She grows even wetter beneath me and I can't help but lift my fingers to my mouth for a taste. I moan at the flavor, so sweet and smokey.

"Fuck," she moans, pulling me to her for a kiss.

We strip our clothes quickly, a mess of fabric piling around us. I have to take a moment when she removes her dress. Creamy, silky skin, and rosebud nipples. Addison is breathtaking. She's curvier than me, her boobs more than twice the size of mine. Her waist dips in tight and I can't help but press my thumbs into the folds of her hips.

Pushing her legs apart, I dip my head low and run my tongue along her slit. Addison arches off the bed with a moan, pinching those rosy nipples as she does. I tease her clit with my tongue, moving in circles with a pin point pressure.

It doesn't take Addison long to come undone beneath me. The noises she makes are low and breathy, they nearly send me over the edge by sound alone. I continue to lick her clit through her orgasm, gentling my movements.

"Come here," she sighs. I let her pull me up next to her. Even though I am much smaller than her, I let her snuggle into my chest, wrapping my arms around her and stroking her hair as she comes down.

Her gentle caresses on my waist are innocent enough, until she turns her head and begins to lap at my nipple. I cry out at the unexpected pleasure.

"Do you like pain?" Addison asks.

"I... I don't know." I think back to when her spark touched my wrist earlier though. That kind of pain had blurred the lines for me.

"Can I try? I'll be gentle." She runs a finger slowly down between my breasts and towards my abdomen as she speaks.

"I liked it when you zapped my wrist." I tell her honestly.

She hums with mischief, her finger sends a bolt into me just below my belly button. It stings, but pleasure blooms on the spot as well. I let out a low whine, my hands tangling in her hair as I kiss her. Another zap shoots through me as I hold her tightly, this one closer to my pussy. I feel the ghost of it in my clit and it has me dripping.

Is this what being with Addison will be like? Electric shocks that send pleasure straight to my core? I really hope so.

Her fingers finally rub against my clit, and I can't help the deep moan that escapes me.

"May I?" She looks at me expectantly and it takes my brain a moment to register that she's asking if she can shock me there.

Do I want her to shock me there? I'm not sure. There is a part of me that's filled with curiosity to find out how that would feel. I decide to be brave.

"Yes," I whimper.

She continues stroking my clit for a bit, working me up before she zaps me. I grip the hair at her nape tight when she does. I cum immediately at the sensation. The pain forcing my pleasure into overdrive. It's the sweetest torture.

My body has never felt more relaxed either, my muscles so overstimulated that they won't listen to my commands to move.

Addison adjusts us so that I am draped over her. She gently takes down my hair from its buns, running her fingers through any tangles. The sensation lulls me into sleep.

Chapter 22

Hyacinth

When we come down to the kitchen the next morning, Riley is already working away in there.

"Morning," he holds out a cup of coffee to me with a bashful smile. "How do you take your coffee, Addison?"

"She likes it super sweet and milky." I answer for her, moving to sit on a bar stool. There's a slight bite in my voice, but I can tell that he's trying to make it up to me.

Riley slides a breakfast bar each in front of us.

"I made you both lunch too..."

"Fine." I sigh, looking up at him with a grin. "I forgive you."

Addison is looking between us with interest.

"It's nice to properly meet you, Riley." She says, taking the proffered coffee from his hands. I'm impressed that she's managed to string a sentence together. I wasn't surprised that Addison is a groggy girl in the morning. She was a silent presence when we were getting ready, the most vocalization she gave being a grunt. I found it adorable.

"Morning!" Samantha chirps, waltzing into the room and holding out her hand to Addison. "I'm Samantha."

They shake hands and we are all left to a slightly awkward silence. Until a bright idea pops into my head.

"Sam? Just so you know, Addison is able to manipulate technology." I gesture towards her 3D printer in the living space.

"Wait. Really?" She excitedly jumps up and down. "Addison, come, come! Let me show you my printer..."

They move into the living room, leaving me alone with Riley.

"Dude..." I start.

"I know, I know. I'm sorry for barging in on you guys."

"Ugh, that's not even the start, Riley." I put my head in my hands for a moment before continuing. "I wasn't with Addison the other night."

"Oh, *oh*." He leans across the counter so we can whisper. "Shit, Hyacinth. I'm so sorry. I totally put my foot in it, didn't I?"

"It's OK, I know you didn't mean to. Just wanted to give you the context." I start to open my bar. "Besides, we sorted things out. I'm just going to date both of them."

"You're *what*?!" He almost shouts, then lowers his voice again. "I'm not one to judge, but don't you think that's a lot? They might both say that they're OK with it. But that's only going to be for so long... I just don't want you to get upset later, babe."

"I think it's different with them... with monsters, I mean. They don't do relationships in the same way that we do."

"OK," he holds my hand across the table. "Just remember that you're not a monster. I don't want you to get hurt because you pretend otherwise."

He does have a point. I need to remember that just because Liliana and Addison are OK with me seeing other people, it doesn't mean that I have to be. But I don't think I could stop seeing either of them, that would cause me more pain.

"You're going to be late for work!" Riley calls over to Samantha.

"But... we were just about to—" Samantha protests.

"It's OK." Addison interrupts, making eye contact with me. "I'll be back around soon. We can work on the printer stuff together with some more time."

Oh, that was definitely meant for me. My chest warms as my heart thumps excitedly. Addison definitely wants to keep seeing me.

She moves back to sit with us in the kitchen, leaning in for a kiss that makes my toes curl.

"Let's finish our coffee and I will drive you to work."

Getting driven around by these monster ladies is getting to my head. I've only had to get the bus once in the last three days.

When we park at a space at the studio, Addison pulls me in for a kiss that leaves me breathless. Again, I find myself wanting to stay in the car and make-out, rather than go into work.

We part ways just inside the door. I excuse myself to use the bathroom as she goes to meet her friends. I need some space real quick to calm myself down before meeting Alex.

I can't wait too long though, I don't want to be late.

It's just me and Alex in the studio today, working on post-production while Flora is at home writing.

"So... how did the date go?" It's the first thing they ask when I enter the room.

Cringing as I set down my satchel, I know I shouldn't have told Alex about the date yesterday. Although, I wouldn't have gotten to take the afternoon off for that incredible sex with Addison. I squirm some, thinking about her electricity, and about how I can't wait for her to do that to me again.

"Hyacinth..." they tease. I guess ignoring them won't work after all.

"It was good." I sigh, "great, even. Thank you for giving me the afternoon off to spend with her."

"And you did, did you?"

"Oh my God, you're insufferable." I giggle, smacking at them with my notebook. "Yes, we spent a lot longer than just lunch together. She made me a really nice picnic and we ate in the park. Then we went back to my place to play video games."

I can feel how flushed my face is, and it makes me hate that I blush so much.

"Video games, huh?"

"Yes. Now stop asking me about it and let's get to work."

"Yes, boss." They joke, saluting me from their seat.

Chapter 23

Liliana

I texted Hyacinth earlier today, but I haven't heard back from her yet. She's probably busy working, I know some of the producers don't allow phone use in their studios.

My mind keeps straying to her and the night we spent together, the morning after. Her flushed face as I fucked her with my tail, the look in her eyes when she realized what I wanted to do. I want to keep making her feel that way, to keep her looking at me like that.

I've kept myself tucked away in my office today, trying to get through this pile of tasks. A knock at my door pulls me from my thoughts. I pick up my phone and check it again, trying to look busy as I tell them to enter.

It's Tabitha, who is late to assist me with some admin that needs doing. She's a sweet girl, not too much older than Hyacinth. She busies herself with the tasks I set out for her and I go back to my emails.

The party I'm planning has been a nightmare. It's an album launch party for a human singer. One week out and I am still struggling to secure the last few vendors. Finding companies that are happy to work an event with both monsters and humans has been the biggest struggle. Even the Fortune Records name isn't enough to sway most of them. It's not a problem that I have had to deal with before, so it's not a walk in the park for me.

Not to mention, the human singer is currently the bane of my existence. She was signed for a three album deal and so I need to just put up with her for the next few years. She goes by Ivy, and I've never met such an entitled brat. She acts as if I work for her.

I rub at my temples, difficult artists aren't a new struggle for me. It's just not something I want to have to deal with at the moment. If I had my way, I would be taking a week or two off work and setting my little omega up in a nest.

She's not going to go into heat until we find our third, though.

"What do you know of Hyacinth?" I ask Tabitha. A little abruptly, if I'm being honest.

"Hyacinth?" She shuffles her papers before turning to look at me properly. "The new girl? Why do you ask?"

"I was assigned as her buddy. I obviously need to see how she is settling in." I say the lie easily. Tabitha is a good age to befriend my Hyacinth. I'm worried that she hasn't made that many new friends in the studio other than her direct coworkers. I know she is obviously seeing another female, but she needs friends too. Tabitha seems nice enough, albeit a bit of a gossip.

"Anyway," I continue. "On that note, you should befriend her. I'm sure she would be happy for the extra company."

"Umm... yeah, OK." She toys with the end of her hair. "It's not that I don't want to be her friend, or anything. I just haven't made an effort. But I'll change that!"

Shit. Now she thinks it's a direct order from her boss.

"No. I just mean if you would like to." I try to soften my voice. "I've just noticed that she hasn't made too many friends yet."

I want to look after Hyacinth in whatever way I can. So that she has a good network of people to support her.

Tabitha finishes up her work pretty quickly after that, and I let her leave without another word. I feel like I fucked that up. I'm not sure how to properly care for a mate, so I'm doing whatever I can think of.

I try to busy myself with planning out the rest of the week leading up to this party. I still need to secure a catering company with an alcohol license who will actually work with me.

A quick knock at my office door is followed by my beautiful mate poking her head inside. She holds up her phone to me.

"Sorry, I only just read your text. I was working in the studio. Do you need me to come back later?"

"Come in and lock the door." I tell her, watching as she nervously fumbles with the lock. She's wearing some loose combat pants with a tiny crop top. When she turns to face me, I can see the graphic on her shirt clearly. I can't help the laugh that blurts out of me at it.

The graphic has some frog drawings on it, with the letters M.I.L.F. On closer inspection, I can see the smaller text underneath: *Man I Love Frogs*.

"Nice shirt." I tell her, still chuckling to myself. Her smile is shy, and I realize that she might be feeling a bit vulnerable. I haven't seen her since I dropped her off yesterday morning.

"I thought you might find it funny," she says. She still stands by the door, so I gesture for her to come to me.

She steps between my open legs, resting her hands on my shoulders as I grip her hips. The sliver of skin showing between her shirt and her pants is such a tease, I trace a finger along it and watch as she squirms with the tickle.

"I'm a little intimidated by you in your office like this," she admits.

Interesting. I wonder if I can play on that a bit. We didn't get into too much of a dynamic the other evening. Now might be a good time to introduce some more kink.

"Is it bad that I like that, little one?"

Her blush is stunning, her tiny freckles standing out on those round cheeks. Hyacinth gives her head a small shake.

"I remember my words," she tells me. "I did some research online about them... and if it's what I think, then I want to try that out some more."

"Good pet," I praise. Her blush deepens even further at my words. "Does my good little omega want to service her alpha?"

"Yes," she nods vigorously. "I have no idea what you mean by service, but it sounds great whatever it is."

"I'll show you." I chuckle. I pull her in for a slow and sensual kiss, letting my tongue explore her mouth. I kiss her until we're both a bit lightheaded.

"On your knees for me, princess." She does so quickly, my little obedient pet. I stroke her hair before cradling her face with my hand. She leans into my hand like a good little pet, eager for my touch.

"Can I use my powers on you, princess?"

Her nod is followed quickly by a throaty moan as I make her clit pulse with pleasure. It's time for her to learn that I can really do this hands free.

"Be a good little pet and make your alpha cum." I command, removing my hand from her face and leaning back in my chair. I'm wearing a looser fit dress today, rather than my usual pant suit. Hyacinth takes advantage of this, pushing the fabric up over my knees so I can open my legs for her.

My tail winds itself around her leg, slowly stroking her. I make sure to concentrate some power there so that the touch gives her pleasure. She whimpers, her head resting against my leg.

"Ah, ah," I chide. "Focus on servicing your alpha."

She nods, getting my skirt up at my hips. Pushing my panties to the side, she buries her face in my pussy. Pleasure floods through me as her soft tongue laps against my clit.

Hyacinth takes her time, slowly building up my orgasm and working me with her tongue.   My powers continue their assault on her pussy, and she whimpers and writhes beneath me.

"That's my girl. Keep tongue fucking your alpha." Her answering moan vibrates against me deliciously. It doesn't take long for her to orgasm from the pleasure I am giving her. But she continues licking me through it.

My pleasure builds at the sight of her kneeling before me. Breath quickening, I grip her hair tightly, pushing her face against my pussy harder as I cum around her tongue.

When I allow her her freedom, she is gasping for air. A delectable smile fills her face, the peaceful glaze of submission in her eyes.

I adjust my clothes back into place. "Come here," I pull her into my lap and stroke her back as she snuggles in.

"You did such a good job. Did you like that?" She nods against my neck where she is nuzzling. It sends a shiver down my spine.

I feel good about that, a short intro to submission for her. From the look in her eyes, I think she enjoyed it too. I'm conscious not to push her too far though, wanting to ease her into all of this.

Last night I did some research of my own. Humans were into dominant and submissive roles, but it was more a conscious lifestyle choice, not a biological response like it is with monsters. Judging by what Hyacinth has told me about her past sexual relationships so far, I think that this is all very new to her.

I feel some responsibility with that, but I am also excited to be the one to show it all to her.

Chapter 24

Hyacinth

I stay snuggled into Liliana's lap as she gets back to work.

"You can stay there, princess." She tells me. "I have some more work to do for this launch party, but I selfishly want to keep you here with me."

"That sounds nice, just staying here." I yawn a little, snuggling closer and playing with Liliana's flowing locks. The colors are more visible in the bright office lighting.

The strands aren't just the deep burgundy that appear at first glance, but a blend of coppers and bright reds too.

I'm totally wiped out after that sex. Liliana barely even touched me. Pleasuring her like that was a treat in itself, but the pulses of power that she was sending to my clit were incredible.

There was also a much more peaceful pleasure found in submitting to her like that. While she did look after me, I knew that she was in control completely.

Even from just kneeling before her, it felt nice to give up control like that. I know that I would have done anything she asked of me in that moment.

It's something I definitely want to explore with Liliana. Addison and I feel more like equals, and I take pleasure in that too. But with Liliana, I know that she is in control, but I think I trust her with that. I'm pretty confident that she wouldn't take advantage of me, that she would look after me.

I had done some searching online about the words she had given me, and I learned that it's called a traffic light system. That it's used in BDSM. I had no idea that that would ever be something I was interested in, but the more I read about it, the more intrigued I became.

Exploring that is something I feel safe to do with Liliana. It's something I would want to explore with Addison too, but I'm not sure yet how that would work. We are both too similar, I think. Although, there is a sweet torture with her electric shocks. I'm sure that's pretty kinky for some people.

Liliana reaches around me as she works, typing emails and taking phone calls. I kind of like that she keeps me on her lap, ready to go if she needs. It's certainly teaching me patience as I look down at her cleavage in this dress. The temptation to reach out and play with them is strong. But she did say that she had work that she needed to get done.

The bits of information that I gather from her calls are troubling, though. It sounds like she's struggling with getting people to work at her party. Once anyone hears that there will be both human and monster attendees, they quickly lose interest. Some even hang up straight away once they realize.

My beautiful succubus is far too successful for people to be hanging up on her. She's literally a leader in PR for a major label. How dare they hang up on her?

It serves as a reminder that I am currently living in a very tiny bubble. That just because me and my coworkers and friends are OK with monsters, most other humans are still just as bigoted.

I'll do my best to cheer up Liliana tonight if she wants to spend her evening with me. I shoot Riley a text asking

him to change Alfred's water and to feed him tonight for
me.

Chapter 25

L*iliana*

Having Hyacinth perched on my lap while I finished up my work was soothing. I felt a sense of peace, knowing that she was safe and protected. I'm not sure that I realized how much that worry had been affecting me.

With her warm body snuggled into me, I was able to get through more work in a few hours than I had been over the last few days. I eventually found a caterer for the party, the only hang up being that they couldn't serve alcohol. Luckily, I know a demon who works in government, one call from him and we had the license. We were going to have to pay a premium to the catering staff, but anything was worth it at this stage.

"OK, I think I'm done." I announce, rubbing at my temples. I needed to get out of this office lighting and away from my screen.

Hyacinth is softly snoring, her thick lashes brushing her cheekbones and her cheek pressed into my boobs to use as a pillow. It's interesting to observe her like this, she is so warm and vibrant, whereas my complexion is much more ashy and cool-toned. We couldn't be more different in appearance. Not that that's something I am unused to, succubi have a unique look, even amongst demons.

It's strange to have company like this. To have someone that I can invite to come home with me, to have dinner with and share my thoughts with. I've been alone for so long now, ever since moving out of my family home for college. College was fun at first, everyone thinking that being a succubus was cool. But they all just wanted me for my powers, not to really make a connection. Certainly not to make friends.

And then after college... being a female in my field meant that I needed to be cut throat. I had to fight to get to the position I am in now. It was worth it in a way, but before Hyacinth came along, I was mated to my job.

I don't think I realized what I was missing out on. But I do now, seeing my little princess curled up to me, fast asleep. This is the catalyst that I needed, to find joy in something other than my career.

"Hyacinth..." I gently nudge her awake, stroking down her back until her eyes blink open. "I'm finished work now, baby."

She leans back, rubbing at her eyes.

"Sorry, I didn't mean to fall asleep."

"Shh... that's OK. I liked having you rest against me." I pull her back into me for a hug. "Do you want to come back to my place tonight? I can get us takeout on the way and we can snuggle some more."

"Mhmm, yes please." She kisses my neck, moving so that she straddles me properly. "I've been dying to touch you though."

It's so difficult not to lean into this, to let her service me more. But I know we will both be more comfortable at home.

"Let me take you home and feed you first, then I promise I will make you feel so good..." I slip my hand up her tiny shirt, letting my fingers brush against her ribs and the edge of her bra.

Hyacinth lets out a whine, and my alpha senses perk up. The need to protect and take care of her is strong. It's oh so difficult not to sit her on the table and fuck her right now.

"Come on, princess." I pick her up with me as I stand, setting her on the floor as I pack away my laptop. She keeps close to me as we leave the room, forgetting her bag which I pick up for her. Wow, she really is needy for me. I'll have to stop for food on the way home, rather than have it delivered. Otherwise we won't have any dinner at all.

Even though I knew it was safer for her, it killed me to leave Hyacinth locked in the car while I picked up our order.

She is tucked up against me on the couch now, eating her noodles and watching reality TV. The whole concept of monster reality TV fascinated her when I mentioned it on the way home, so here we are. It's a polyamorous dating show, and while overly complicated, it might actually be quite informative for Hyacinth to watch.

"We need to get you watching a human show, because this is great!" She gushes, munching on a spring roll. She's adorable when she's excited like this, or when she finds something new she's passionate about.

"If I must…" I pretend to look annoyed, but I know she can see right through me.

We start another episode. It's not too late, and I want to give her a moment to rest before we have sex. I have ideas for this evening. I tuck my wing around her as she gets comfy.

"Did you fix the issue with the caterer?" She asks, surprising me. I guess she was listening to my calls.

"I did." I kiss the top of her head, mussing up her hair. "We officially have a caterer with a temporary alcohol license. So that's a big task off my plate."

"That's great! I hope you don't mind me listening in, though."

"Of course not." I'm quite flattered that she paid attention, that she cared about my work.

Hyacinth doesn't wait until the episode is finished. We have about ten minutes left when she turns over, her hand roaming my body as she pulls me in for a kiss. She strokes my horns and then my wings, drawing deep moans from my throat. Her delicate touch on my wings feels exquisite, nearly as good as her rubbing against my clit.

Pulling her closer against me, I whisper in her ear.

"Do you trust me?"

She nods fervently, writhing against me. I pick her up and stand in one swift movement, taking us to my bedroom.

"Don't move." I command, setting her down in the center of the bed. She whimpers as I pull away, but she does as she's told.

Rooting through my drawer of toys, I pull out some bondage rope. I won't push her too far in the toy department tonight, but I will be tying her up. If she lets me.

Sitting on the bed next to her, I keep some distance so I can have her full attention. She looks nervously between me and the rope in my hands.

"What's that for?" Hyacinth gulps, her teeth grazing her lips.

"I'm going to tie you up, if you'd like." Hyacinth moves closer to me, her hand running over the rope, testing its texture. I lean in close, speaking in low tones. "Then I'm going to have my way with you. You can scream at me to stop, but I won't unless you say your words. Do you understand, pet?"

"Yes. I understand." Her brown orbs meet my gaze. I search them to see if she is being genuine, that she's prepared for this. There is a hesitancy there, but it's mixed with a level of trust that I feel honored to have.

"Get up and take off your clothes for me, then." My little Hyacinth is shy, and I know it might be a little cruel to have her strip for me. But I am obsessed with the tiny shake to her hands, the stumble as she tries to get her feet out of her pants.

"Wait. Let me look at you for a minute." I say, when her pants are off. She wears only her tiny crop top and her high rise briefs. They both hit her waist and create a sinful shape.

"Turn around and show me your ass." Her full cheeks are on display, and I can't help but reach out and grab one in each hand. "Bend over," I command, squeezing her there. I give her a gentle smack, gripping hard on the impact so it's not too painful. She whimpers, the sound going straight to my pussy.

My tail traces up her leg and over her hip, the tip threading under the waistband of her panties. I let it travel up further and under her shirt to graze against her nipples. The tip of my tail is another pleasure point for me, and I can't help the moan that escapes me at the feel of her pert nipple against it.

"Stand back up, arms above your head." I take pleasure in removing her shirt for her. "Arms back down again, princess."

I'm giving her simple commands to follow, helping her get into a state of submission. Removing her bra, I can't help but taste her nipple, sucking on it until I draw a cry from her.

"Stay there." I move back to the bed, picking up and beginning to unravel the discarded rope. Now, how will I tie her up? I assess her from my perch, her plump little ass on display. Hmm... I want to see her face as she cums for me though.

"Just relax for me, baby." I whisper in her ear from behind. Her answering shiver is so fucking sexy. I have to take a deep breath and remember to be patient.

I twist her arms outwards, keeping them flat against her torso. Then I start the process of wrapping the rope around her. I frame her boobs with the rope, tying her upper arms in place. Once she's secure, I step away and admire my handiwork. Hyacinth's breaths are coming quicker, her scent strengthening with her arousal. Her face is flushed, her eyes glazed over with the security of the ropes.

"You look beautiful," I slip her panties off completely and guide her to lay back on the bed, her feet still flat on the floor. "That's it, scoot up a bit and get comfy." I raise one of her legs, resting her foot on my shoulder as I wrap the rope just above her knee. Lifting her arm, I tie her wrist to her leg.

Repeating the same steps on the other side, she's bared before me. Her dripping pussy is on full display, her legs pushed back and resting against her arms. In this position, she can't close her legs at all, they're fixed in place. She could attempt to wriggle away from me, and she can move her head. Otherwise, she's trapped.

I can feel my pussy getting slick, seeing her like this before me. The things I want to do to her...

"Is that comfortable?" I ask, checking in.

"Yes. Well, it doesn't hurt." I chuckle, moving around the bed and back to my drawer of toys.

"Just let me know if you get pins and needles, or if any of your limbs go to sleep. Say orange so I know what you mean. OK?"

"OK."

I open my drawer, moving around its contents and deciding what she might be open to me using. While I can make my tongue and my tail vibrate, I do like to use them for other things as well. A vibrating wand will drive her crazy. That's what I grab, along with some lube.

When I turn, I see that she's twisted her head to watch me. Her eyes straining to see what I'm up to. I let her see the vibrator, the widening of her eyes worth the reveal.

Moving back to the bed, I rest the wand on her stomach. I switch through the settings, letting her feel the possibilities of what might be ahead of her.

"Do you want this on your pussy?" I ask, switching it back to the lowest setting.

"Yes, please." She nods, her little tongue darting out to lick her plush rosy lips.

"Have you ever used a vibrator before?"

She shakes her head. Fuck. The way I am going to blow my little Hyacinth's mind tonight.

I gently trail the wand down her stomach, finally hitting her clit and resting there. She cries out, her muscles straining as she tries to pull away. I see the panic in her eyes when it really hits her. That she can't move, that I can do whatever I want with her.

I pull the device away, leaving it to rest on the bed next to her, still buzzing away. The rope makes it back into my hands and I start to wrap it along one of her thighs. The vibrator is in my hands again, and I settle it against her clit. I watch her responses to see where it is most sensitive. Then I hold it in place as I attach it to the rope tied to her leg.

I'm impressed with my handiwork, that vibrator is going nowhere. Hyacinth is whimpering, crying out my name, as the vibrator keeps pulsing at her clit. She's beginning to come undone now, her skin slick with sweat, her cheeks a permanent flush. It's fucking beautiful.

I keep in her line of vision as I start to strip. I ease off my panties, but I keep my black, lacy bra on.

Crawling on to the bed next to Hyacinth, I put my head close to hers.

"Please..." She whimpers. "Please, Liliana... I—" She cries out, the moan a high pitch as she orgasms on the vibrator. I keep my eyes on her the whole time, watching as she realizes that it's not stopping. The vibrations continue against her clit as she starts to protest. Her body is twitching, trapped in place and forced to ride out her orgasm for longer through the intense vibrations.

"Please what, baby?" I chuckle. "You're only on the lowest setting... be a good girl and I won't have to turn it up on you."

I sit up and swing my leg over her so I am sitting against her chest.

"Now be a good omega and lick your alpha's clit." I move forward, pressing my pussy against her face.

Her little tongue darts out immediately, her moans causing a vibration of their own against my clit. I thrust against her face, grinding my clit against her and limiting her breathing. In this position, she can't see what I'm doing as I reach for the lube.

I cover the tip of my tail, making sure it is nice and slick. My tail moves to her entrance, slowly sliding in and filling up my omega.

The warmth of her walls against my tip feels amazing. Combined with the oral she's giving me, it doesn't take long for me to orgasm. My breath heaving, I move off of her.

My tail stays inside my little Hyacinth, and now that I can concentrate better, I start to fuck her with it.

The movement against her G-spot sends her over the edge for the second time. I decide to show her some mercy, stilling my tail and switching off the vibrator.

The room is almost silent without the incessant buzzing. The only sounds are her heavy breaths and whimpers. With the absence of any friction, she whines, grinding against the still wand.

"Awh… does my poor baby need some friction?" I tease her nipples with my fingers as she whimpers again. "I need to hear you speak, pet."

"Mhmm… please. Please make me cum again." She continues to writhe against the vibrator.

I will give it to her, but I will drive her crazy in the process.

"If you insist." I switch the vibrator back on and she screams, her poor clit is probably so sensitive now. She didn't know what she was asking for. Switching up through the settings, I find the one I'm looking for.

It's a slow build from a very low to high speed vibration. Just when you feel like you're about to cum, it switches back to the low vibration and starts all over again. It's torturous.

Every time, I see her tense, like it's about to happen. By the third time that it goes back to the low vibration, she groans in frustration.

"Please!"

I ignore her, deciding to add on to the torture. I thrust my tail inside her, matching the pace with the vibrations, speeding up with it and stopping when it moves again to the low setting.

A choked sob escapes Hyacinth, a loose tear escaping her eye.

"Please... ah—" she moans again. "Please, please, please..."

She chants at me as I keep up the pace now, fucking her harder and faster with my tail. This time when the vibrator builds, I switch it to the steady setting on the highest mode.

Hyacinth screams, her pussy clenching my tail as she rides out the longest orgasm. Once I feel like she's had enough, I switch the vibrator off. Her pussy continues clenching around my tail, and I have to hold on to the bed frame from the pleasure of it. I reach down, rubbing my own clit. My pussy is slick, my fingers moving easily, and I make myself cum again as she squeezes my tail.

I pull my tail free from her and watch as her pussy clenches around nothing, her thighs spread wide for me to see.

"How many more do you have for me?"

Chapter 26

Hyacinth

Taking the bus home feels a bit weird, even though it's only been a few days since I was last on one.

Last night was incredible. Liliana made me cum so many times I lost count. By the end of it all, I was an incoherent mess.

She had gently untied me and helped me to stretch out my muscles. Then she ran me a bubble bath and relaxed my body with a massage. She even wrapped me up in some cozy pajamas that she bought for me to keep at her place.

Another night was spent curled up in one of my monsters arms and it was so nice. It will be weird to be in my bed alone tonight.

Today at work was another story though. Flora was in such a weird mood and maybe a bit down? She just wasn't herself. But Alex had signaled for me to not mention it. At one point he discreetly told me to give her some space to work through it. So I kept my mouth shut.

Flora got us takeout for lunch though, which was great. We ate together and had a bit of fun, chatting about a new movie that was coming out as part of a larger series.

I didn't see Addison at the studio today though. I was tempted to text her, but I also wanted to leave the ball in her court. She might need some space after Riley's comment and my complete idiocy.

I get home quicker than I expect. I finished up a bit early today, so I managed to avoid the evening rush of traffic.

My room feels smaller now, somehow. Everything in my life is just a bit off when I'm not around either Addison or Liliana. Like my center of gravity has shifted.

My first point of call is to give Alfred a bit of love. I've neglected his tank for a few days now, so I give the substrate a good clean before feeding him.

A knock sounds at my door.

"Come in!" I call, my hands busy with the tank mainte-nance.

"I knocked!" Riley praises himself as he strolls in. "See? I'm learning."

I huff at him, but it's in a joking way.

"Samantha will be home soon, and I was thinking of taking the night off from studying so we could all hang out?"

That does sound nice. It's been a hot minute since we got to hang out, just the three of us.

"Are you cooking dinner?" I tease, pretending that he's going to have to work to convince me.

"Mhmm, I was thinking of making Kung Pao chicken with pak choi. We also have a new board game that I picked up earlier..."

"Well, in that case, you do need me. There's no way you'll be able to make sense of the instructions yourself."

"Exactly!" He leans in, giving me a quick forehead peck before leaving and shutting the door behind him.

It was fun, but I think I'm done giving him a hard time now. He obviously didn't mean to say that to Addison, and it was my fault for not telling her sooner.

After an hour or so of doing chores and catching up on life, I join Samantha and Riley in the living space. Riley has plated up some Kung Pao chicken, as promised.

"So…" Samantha starts, as we settle on the floor around the coffee table. "Tell us everything!"

"Yeah, who were you with last night…?!" Riley adds.

"God, let a girl eat her dinner!" I laugh though, and I tell them about everything that has been going on with my love life. I leave out the details of the sex, more so just explaining what we've been up to.

"I know Riley is going to say something about being careful… but honestly, Cinthi? I'm glad you're having fun. I think this is good for you. You can be free, you deserve it."

"I already told her that, actually." Riley quips. "But honestly, as long as you're happy, then we're happy to hear all about these monster dates!"

We share a giggle, pulling out the new board game. I have to take the lead on explaining everything, as per usual. But it's nice, it's fun to hang out just the three of us on a Friday night.

We stay up late, the weekend ahead of us free of any responsibilities. I am looking forward to my couple of days off from work.

Chapter 27

*H*yacinth

I roll over in my bed, the light streaming in working in tandem with the buzzing sound. Both things clearly were trying to ruin my morning.

Pulling the sheets over my head, at least one of the problems is solved. The annoying buzzing hasn't though, and I become just lucid enough to realize that it's my phone.

Scrambling to pick it up, I knock it off my nightstand and it falls on the floor. The buzzing stops, and I almost turn back over and go back to sleep. Begrudgingly, I reach down to pick it up off the floor.

1 Missed Call ☐*Liliana Whitcombe*

Liliana called me?! Who calls people, anyway? I quickly dial her back, putting it on speaker and resting it on the pillow next to my head.

"Morning, princess."

"Morning." I grumble. "Sorry I missed you, I thought my phone was trying to attack me."

"Oh, did I wake you?" She chuckles lightly. It's cute to hear, and I find myself cheering up. "I wanted to take you out for breakfast this morning. But if you're too sleepy..."

"Wait..." I blink rapidly, trying to wake myself up. "Breakfast sounds nice. Do I have time to get ready?"

"Of course. I'll start driving to yours now. But don't rush, I was just playing with you. Take your time."

I breathe a sigh of relief. I get panicked pretty easily in my sleepy state.

"Hang on," my mind is clearing up now. "Where are we going? Where is there that we can both go together?"

"I have an idea, if you're comfortable with it. I thought we could go to a nice hotel, they are very upscale, so they wouldn't let anything bad happen." She pauses for a moment. "I wouldn't let anything bad happen to you either, princess."

"Will my big scary succubus protect me?" I put on a fake baby voice. "I'm not worried. Breakfast at a fancy hotel sounds like a great way to kick off my weekend."

We chat some more before hanging up. Liliana to start the drive to get me, and me to figure out what the hell I'm going to wear.

I quickly rinse off, but I don't have time to wash my hair. So I spray some dry shampoo on the roots and pull it back into one long braid. I never wear my hair in anything other than my signature space buns. But it could be nice to try something new today.

I hadn't realized how long my hair had gotten lately, the end of my braid hitting my shoulder blades. I quickly put lotion on my legs and start to dig in my wardrobe to find something nice enough to wear to a fancy hotel.

I'm too small to borrow anything of Samantha's, so I decide to save her the wake up call. What did she have me wear to that weird date brunch? Oh, yes, the pinafore. OK, so that's kind of the vibe. I have another dress that I usually wear in the winter, layered with a roll neck. I eventually find it hiding in the back.

It's a burnt orange color, with a low neckline and a fitted waist. I toss it on, picking out some gold sandals and gold jewelry to layer. For my makeup, I put on a flick of Kohl along my outer lash line, to dress up my usual look. I also add a touch of gold shimmer to my inner corners.

I look different, with my hair pulled back like this, and the new style of makeup. It's a slight change, but it makes me feel a bit more grown up. I also really like this orange color on me. Normally, I would have it layered over something else, but the color straight up against my brown skin works really well.

My phone buzzes with a text, and I assume it's from Liliana to say she is outside. Instead, it's Addison's name that highlights my screen.

Can I take you on a date tonight? I figure I can get away with looking human enough to take you somewhere nice.

I squeal a little. Yes! I was hoping she would text. I giddily text back that I will see her then. She'll easily be able to fit in on the human side of the city, especially if she's with me.

This time when my phone buzzes, it's Liliana.

I'm outside, I'll wait in the car. Can't wait to see you x

My heart warms, my stomach fluttering with butterflies. I can't wait to see her either. I quickly put all my things in a purse, rather than taking my work satchel. I top up my lip gloss one more time before heading downstairs to see my succubus.

I drop my keys trying to lock the front door behind me, and I blush at my stumble. I giggle as I get into the car.

Liliana is perfect. She is dressed slightly more relaxed then she usually does for work. Her hair is combed over to one side, her profile stunning even in the dim light of the cloudy morning. She's wearing a light, summery blouse tucked into a long, pleated skirt. It's nice to see her in something softer like this. Although, I do love her structured suits.

"You look beautiful," she tells me. And I realize that we have both been silently taking in one another. There's a hunger in her gaze, but she gives me a chaste kiss on the cheek. "I don't want to mess up your lip gloss."

"You look beautiful, too." Ugh, I couldn't come up with an original compliment?

We chat on the drive, Liliana telling me about the party planning and how it's coming along. I tell her about my evening with my friends, and how it was fun to just hang out and play games.

"I'd like that," she suggests. There's a hesitancy in her voice that I'm not used to from her. "A game night with your friends, I mean. It would be good to meet some other humans outside of the studio, too."

"That could be arranged." I tell her. It would be weird to see Liliana in a relaxed setting like that. But I am also dying to see her let her hair down around other people like she does with me.

We pull up to the hotel and it is *fancy*. There's a valet who takes the car keys from Liliana as we get out. He's another demon, I think, with dark gray skin and bat like wings.

She holds out her arm to me, so I put my hand in the crook of her elbow and follow her up the steps to the entrance. Her wing twitches protectively around me, and I relax some.

It's just a restaurant. If anyone has an issue with me, that doesn't mean they'll try to hurt me. Besides, with witches like Addison who look mostly human, who's to say that I'm not a monster, anyway?

Everyone, it seems. I stand out, many heads turning to get a glance of me as we walk through the lobby.

"Don't worry, princess." Liliana soothes, patting my hand. "They're just curious. I can sense emotions, so I would know otherwise. OK?"

I nod slowly, my heart rate speeding up as I see a naga, but he's not like Aspis from the studio. This naga has a hood, like a cobra, growing from his middle back, flaring out at his shoulders, and meeting again at the top of his head. I shiver, the slithering way he moves making me feel unsettled.

Liliana steers me away from him and towards the restaurant. The head waiter is another demon, who happily welcomes us and brings us to a table with a pretty view of a garden outside.

"Do you only go to establishments run by demons?" I ask, once the waiter has left us to look over the menus.

"When I'm with you? Yes." She chuckles, glancing down at the options. "I can trust other demons to respect that you are my guest. We have a sort of 'code of conduct', and they would never allow harm to come to you."

"Oh." Well, that was kind of nice. I can't imagine any group of humans really having each other's back like that.

We chat a bit more over our food, I get the most delicious eggs Benedict of my life. It's nice and relaxed, the restaurant never getting too busy.

We order another round of coffee once we're done eating. I'm not in any rush to go anywhere, I want to lap up whatever time I have with my succubus today.

The summer heat is sweltering, and I have both windows in our living space wide open, hoping for a lick of a breeze.

Breakfast with Liliana was so lovely. Afterwards, she dropped me back home again, leaving me with a sensual kiss in the car.

It was nice for us to spend time together without any sexual expectations. And I think that's what Liliana was going for with the date. I learned so much more about her life and her family. Turns out her Dad is a pretty big guy in the demon community, another reason why they're all super respectful of me.

What surprised me the most was how easy it was, being around that many monsters. They definitely knew I was a human, but nobody bothered us at all.

Something tells me that it wouldn't be the same if Liliana were to join me for breakfast in the human side of the city.

Samantha joined me to watch some TV when I first got home. I debriefed her on my morning and we had some snacks and gossiped. By gossiped, I mean that she caught me up on some creator drama from people that she follows online.

The doorbell rings, and it's a jarring sound that I'm not used to. I quickly bounce up off the couch and grab my bag on the way. Addison is early, but I'm not mad about it at all.

"Hey, little one." She kisses me to say hello. If it wasn't for the heat, I'd be skipping dinner and bringing her to my bed. I'm instantly horny, my thighs clenching together, as she pulls me closer by my neck. I'm panting by the time we part.

I'm glad I changed into some cutoffs and a crop top, the summer really has kicked in with this heat. Addison is wearing a low cut tank, tucked into a pleated mini skirt. I can almost see her ass, her skirt is so short.

Her hips sway as we walk to the car, and I really have to hold myself back from grabbing her ass in the middle of my driveway. Her hair is pulled back into a ponytail, and it swishes back and forth as she walks, too. She's topped off her look with a baseball cap, and it works to make her look more Human.

"There's a taco place not far from here that I thought we could go to." I suggest.

"Perfect! Yes, I had forgotten about the whole 'picking somewhere to eat' thing." Her tinkling laugh fills the car. The A/C switches on with the engine, and I immediately moan at the blissful feeling of the cool air on my body.

"Your hair is pretty in a braid like that," she says as I input the address to the restaurant on her phone.

I blush, happy that both of my females complimented my hair today. Maybe I should try different styles more often.

The taco place is busy, but I think that serves us well. We both go pretty much unnoticed, even the staff forgetting our table a couple times. It's perfect.

We order tacos in rounds, so we can chill and keep our table for longer. Addison is driving, so we try out some of the special sodas on offer and it washes down my barbacoa perfectly.

After a final round of guacamole and chips, I lean back in my chair and pat my belly.

"I think I'm done." I groan, accepting defeat.

"Me too." She agrees. "I'm gonna need a minute before I can make it back to the car."

"Did you want to stay over tonight?" I mentally kick myself for the hopeful note in my voice. I need to get better at playing it cool.

"Oh, I thought that was a given." I'm delighted by her tinkling laugh again. "I even brought an overnight bag."

Chapter 28

Addison

We barely make it inside the front door before my lips are on her. Hyacinth's leg hooks around my hip as I press her against the wall. Kissing her neck as she writhes against me, her hands grip at my nape.

A noise sounds from further inside the house, and I come to my senses. I had forgotten that other people might be here.

"Let's go straight up to my room," she suggests, hooking a finger in the waistband of my skirt.

"Addison!" Samantha comes barreling into the hallway, hardly noticing the position Hyacinth and I just jumped out of. "I didn't know you were coming over tonight."

She gives a pointed look to Hyacinth.

"I wish I had known you guys were coming back, I definitely would have wanted to hang. But Nick is coming to pick me up soon and I am going over to his place tonight."

I don't know who Nick is, but I'm not disappointed that Samantha will be gone. She's nice and all, and I am sure I would like her if I got the chance to know her better. But right now, all I want is to have Hyacinth whimpering beneath me on her bed.

"Is Riley not home?" Hyacinth answers for me. Which is good, because I am kind of just awkwardly standing here at this point.

"No, he decided to visit his parents tonight."

"Oh yeah, he had mentioned that."

The pair chat a bit, but I can't help but focus my attention on my little human. I hook my finger in the belt loop of her cut offs, right in the center of her back. Tugging her towards me, I try to signal that I need these off and on her floor.

"Well, we're gonna head up then." She finally announces, and we move past Samantha. I try to give her a pleasant smile, but I feel like it might have just looked pained.

"Don't you want your bag?" Samantha asks, reaching down to grab it and holding it out to me.

"Oh shit, yeah. Thanks Samantha." I take it from her quickly, Hyacinth half dragging me down the hallway.

She stumbles up the stairs in her haste.

"You're clumsy when you're eager." I tease, playfully pinching her butt.

She squeals, swatting my hand away, running up the last few steps. I follow her into the room and shut the door behind me. Dumping my bag on the floor, I prowl towards Hyacinth, who backs up until her knees hit the bed and she falls flat on her ass.

I grip her by the waist, stepping between her legs. She pulls me down to kiss her, our tongues tangling as we devour one another. I briefly break our kiss to pull her shirt over her head. Her shorts are off next, underwear following quickly until she's completely bare before me.

Fuck.

I drop to my knees, pulling her towards me and settling her legs on my shoulders. The earthy vetiver of her scent is stronger here, along with a hint of musk.

I kiss and bite along the inside of her thigh, pausing when I reach her pussy. The slickness is prominent already.

I'm proud that I can make her wet like this, that she wants me as much as I want her.

Leaning in for a taste, my eyes roll back with how good it is. It's tough to pull away, but I have something I want to try with her.

"Can I use a toy with you?" I ask.

"Mhmm," she whimpers. "I don't have anything, though."

"I do." I go back to where I dumped my bag at the door. "I brought something with me."

Pulling out the dildo, I turn to see Hyacinth splayed out on the bed, rubbing her own clit as she watches me. There's a smile on her lips as she pulls one between her teeth.

"You're so fucking sexy, Hyacinth." I can't help but suck on one of her perfect boobs, my teeth grazing gently.

I hold up the glass dildo in my hand to show her. It's nothing too big, but it's what I can do with it that is special.

"Get this nice and wet for me." Placing the tip at her lips, I watch as Hyacinth takes it into her mouth. She sucks and licks the smooth glass, and I fuck her mouth with it to make sure it's plenty wet.

I move back onto my knees on the floor, "Can I still use my powers on you?"

"Yes," she whimpers. There's a hitch of nervousness in her voice. "But with the toy? What are you going to do?"

"Better to show you." The dildo easily slips into her, and I moan at the sight of it easing into her pussy. I fuck her with it for a bit, helping to build up her arousal. Tonguing her clit as well, she becomes a whimpering mess beneath me.

When she's chanting my name over and over, that's when I add the electricity. It takes a bit more focus to get a small current like this going. I still the motion of the dildo inside her, pushed in all the way.

With the right level of current, the electricity will make her muscles contract in a pulsing pattern. She cries out, and I feel like I will die if I don't touch myself to that sound. I shove my skirt up and dip my hand into my panties. My fingers meet a pool of wetness and they easily glide over my clit. Humping my hand, I increase the current in Hyacinth's pussy. I watch her pussy closely to monitor how she reacts... there.

The dildo moves back and forth as her walls contract around it. It's much easier on my concentration levels to just keep it steady now.

"Fuck!" Hyacinth hardly ever cusses around me, and I love the sound of it. To know I have worked her up to that point. I stand up, stripping off my clothes and climbing over her. I straddle her hips and lean down to kiss her.

Her hands roam my body, landing on my ass and pulling me closer to her. My wet pussy presses against her stomach and the friction is delicious. I can tell she's cresting closer to her orgasm, as she struggles to focus on kissing, her head tipping back against the sheets.

I increase the current ever so slightly, to help her out, concentrating the energy where I think her G-spot is. Going silent, she fists the sheets, back arching, eyes squeezing shut. It's so fucking beautiful.

"That's it," I coax. "Cum for me, Hyacinth."

The sound that she makes as she cums makes me hornier than I think I've ever been. I slide off of her, mentally lowering the current in the dildo. I slowly pull it out of her, setting it on the floor.

It's going to take some time for her muscles to stop twitching. So I pull her up onto the bed fully, and tuck her into my arms.

"That was..." She tries to speak, but just buries her head in my neck instead. Using an arm around my waist to pull me closer to her.

I stroke her back, her arms, trying to soothe and relax her. Every once in a while she twitches, her body convulsing with the after effects of her orgasm.

"Fuck, Addison." She finally pulls away enough to kiss me. It's filled with emotion, and I try to communicate my feelings back to her. I am obsessed with this little human. It feels so right to be snuggled up with her.

Although, there is a lingering feeling in the back of my head that we're not complete. Yet.

Chapter 29

Addison

Monday mornings are generally disgusting. But nothing sucks more than coming into work to find out that your coworker has taken the day off without telling you. Apparently Sebastian has been pulled for some PR bullshit today.

Which is fine, but how did I find out? Not from fucking Sebastian. No, his girlfriend just happened to run into me in the break room to tell me.

Flora is covered in his scent, it's almost sickening. But she seems happy, relaxed and content. I'm sure Hyacinth stinks of me, too. The humans are lucky that they can't smell things like this. Heck, I'm lucky I'm not a shifter... those guys can *smell*.

My phone chimes with a text from Sebastian. It's pretty apologetic, so I feel a bit better.

I spot Hyacinth in the hallway, chatting with Tabitha. A plan strikes me.

"Hey guys," I say, rushing to catch them in the hallway before they come into the break room. "Tabitha! Looks like Flora has a bit of time to kill today. She was just telling me a really interesting piece of gossip..."

"Ooh," she takes the bait. "Excuse me, ladies."

I hold Hyacinth's arm, preventing her from following her.

"I'm getting you some free time, come on."

Finding an empty studio, I pull Hyacinth in, locking the door behind us. I lift her onto the desk, recreating our first kiss as I step between her legs. She grinds against me, her fingers fisting in my hair as she kisses me.

We moan and writhe against each other. I know that we don't have more than a few minutes alone, but of course I use it to work us both up into a frenzy.

I palm her boob through her shirt, earning myself a delightful moan from my human. Pinching her nipple hard, that moan turns into a cry. God, I can't wait until I get to fuck her again. I still haven't gotten to lick her clit until she cums all over my face.

I kiss down her neck, so that I can hear her breathy moans more clearly.

A knock sounds at the door, and I groan, pressing my head against hers. They can wait a second. I peck her lips once more, a quick and comforting embrace, before straightening myself up.

Hyacinth just stays in place, panting heavily, her eyes focused on me with a pained expression.

"I'll make it up to you." I promise, pulling her to standing and straightening her up too before I unlock the door.

It's Flora and Alex on the other side.

"Oh hey guys," I move aside to let them in. "I was just catching up with Hyacinth, she had a question on something tech related. Didn't realize the door had locked itself, weird."

I look back to see Hyacinth trying to look busy. It's adorable. When she looks up at me, I give her a secret wink, watching the blush spread across her cheeks.

"Anyway, see you guys later!" I stride out the door and leave them to fill in the blanks themselves. I hope they don't question her too much.

Chapter 30

Liliana

A quick text to Hyacinth and she's in my office, straddling my lap, in less than ten minutes. I could get used to this.

"Flora isn't coming in today," she explains. "And Alex was a little pissed about the song she released. So they didn't even notice that I slipped out. They need their space right now, anyway."

She arches against me, giving me a slow and loving kiss. Loving? That's what it feels like though. I know that Hyacinth is mine, and I do think that my feelings are strong enough to be love. I don't think I should bring that up, though.

"That song is going to either be a big win, or be a complete disaster from a PR perspective." I say, when she pulls away. "It's good, though."

"It's so good." She agrees. "Although, I know that both of their production teams could have elevated it a bit. But I'm biased."

Her giggle is adorable, but it swiftly turns to a moan as I start kissing her neck.

"How is the party going?" she asks.

"It's crunch time," I sigh. "Now we're onto the finer details. I'm going to be pretty busy in the lead up."

Disappointment shows on her face, before she tries to cover it up with an encouraging smile. I absentmindedly wrap my tail around her leg in soothing strokes. My alpha instincts are screaming at me to do whatever it takes to make her comfortable, to keep her with me permanently. But I know that I can't do that. The best way that I can provide for her is by doing well in work and keeping a good income.

"Can I go to the party...?"

"Of course! Everyone in the label is invited to these events, princess." I stroke her cheek gently. "I know you're still seeing someone else at the label, so I wouldn't force it on you as a date. Besides, I won't be much fun while I'm getting everything set up."

She nods, absentmindedly playing with the ends of my hair. Something is troubling her, I can tell. But I also know that she would tell me if she wanted to talk about it.

I pull her into another kiss, letting her lose herself in it. Hoping that it helps.

Chapter 31

Hyacinth

I've enlisted Samantha and Riley's help with getting ready this evening. We went shopping after work the other day and got me a new dress, too.

"You're going to look so hot, Cinthi!" Samantha is the ultimate hype girl in these situations.

I actually took the time to properly style my curls today, leaving them down. They are almost long enough to cover my boobs now... I really need a haircut. Samantha twisted some pieces back, but left a couple face framing strands loose. It creates a nice cascading effect that looks pretty.

We chat while I do my makeup, and she catches me up with all things Nick.

"Yeah, so the other night when he came to pick me up, he said he'd prefer to just stay here. But I mentioned that you had someone over, so obviously I had promised you an empty house. Right?"

"Right," I nod along. I decide to contour my face, chiseling my jawline.

"So obviously I made him drive me to his place." She flicks her hair over her shoulder. "He never asked me about who you had over or anything, we just hung out like usual for the weekend.

"But anyway, you know that I stayed back to meet him on Tuesday at the mall?"

"Yeah," I wonder where she's going with this.

"Well, he said he had been chatting to Chris. You know, the guy I forced you to date."

"How could I forget?" I pause to giggle before going back to applying my blush.

"Well he was all, 'Chris said Hyacinth was looking at monsters on her phone that day and that's why he didn't want to get with her'." She exaggerates a male voice as she imitates Nick. "And I was all, yeah, well, she works with them… he was shocked! And I was like, don't you listen to anything I say? Because I have definitely told him that you're working with monsters.

"Anyway, he got really weird about it, and asked if I had spoken with any of them. And I was like, yeah, obviously. I told him about Addison and how she has been over a couple of times."

I've stopped with my makeup now, turning to look at Samantha in shock.

"He freaked, Cinthi. Made a big scene in the mall and everything. Turns out he is not a fan of monsters. But like, I'm glad I found out now. So I broke up with him."

She says it so nonchalantly, playing with the ends of her hair.

"Wait, what?" It takes me a second to really understand what she's saying. "Sam! Are you OK?"

I hop up, pulling her into a hug. "Why didn't you say anything?"

"I think I just wanted to process on my own. Because, fuck him. You know?"

"Yeah, of course."

Riley chooses that moment to join us, drinks in hand to help me get buzzed before the party. He sets them down on my desk when he sees us hugging. He joins the huddle, wrapping his arms around both of us.

"Why are we hugging?" He asks in a hushed tone.

Samantha explains everything to him too and it sombers the mood. She shakes her head, laughing at us and telling us she's fine. We put on some music and try to have some fun.

I look in the mirror once I'm ready. The tight black dress hugs my boobs and ass. The low 'v' showing a lot more skin than I am used to. I wear my go to layered necklaces for when I'm trying to dress up. Samantha pulls out some of my old bangles to wear too, and I'm ready.

Well, except the high heels that they made me buy. I'm nervous about trying to walk in them.

Chapter 32

L*iliana*

The party has been a success so far. I didn't realize how anxious I was about the vendors actually showing up and working until they did. Luckily, things seem to be going well.

I surprisingly have a smile on my face as I leave the bathroom. The room full of people enjoying themselves, the sound of Ivy's new album playing over the speakers. I feel accomplished.

It's weird to think that I actually have someone to share that with now. Speaking of, I spot Hyacinth across the room, leaning against the bar. Her beautiful curls are down tonight. Wow, she looks stunning in that black dress, legs for days in those heels. I want to wear them like a necklace.

I stand and watch her for a moment, her skin glowing under the lights. She really does look amazing. She laughs at something and the happiness in her eyes makes me melt. A male had been blocking my view of who she was talking to, but he moves now. A shock of violet hair is visible.

Surely not?

My chest hurts as I see Addison caressing my mate's face like a lover would. Hyacinth looks up at her and a blush forms on her cheeks. My blush. The blush that she wears for *me*, that *I* try to coax from her.

Panic fills me for the first time about all of this. I have to turn away, trying to calm down my alpha instincts. I move back into the hallway, the party feeling suffocating all of a sudden. There's no way that Addison is our third... right?!

That ship has long since sailed.

Oh God, Addison can't be our mate... I would know it. This ruins *everything*. Poor Hyacinth seemed so happy there too. I can't imagine having to deal with her heartbreak if she is faced with choosing between us.

Hyacinth probably doesn't feel mating in the same way that we monsters do. She'll have no way of really knowing that I'm her mate over Addison.

I startle as small and soft arms wrap around my waist from behind. Relaxing into her hold, I turn to face Hyacinth.

"The party is great," she tells me. She's never felt smaller or more fragile in my arms. I can't let her go. "I noticed that you saw me and Addison... you didn't look OK so I wanted to come check up on you."

Hyacinth's big doe eyes look up at me with compassion, but I see worry there too. I know I'm going to have to be honest with her.

"I saw that you looked really sad, Liliana." She continues. "I feel guilty, I don't want you to be upset. I knew that it was a bad idea to keep seeing you both."

She starts to tear up, and I come to my senses. I shush her, "It's on me, not on you. Addison and I just have a bit of history, that's all.

"Come on." I pull her out a side door into an alleyway so we can have some fresh air.

The coolness of the air is calming against my skin.

"Let me explain." I keep my distance from Hyacinth while I speak. "Addison and I met four or five years ago, when she and Sebastian were just getting started. She was young, but I was younger then too. I'm not the good person in this story, Hyacinth.

"I was attracted to her, initially. I thought that I needed to be harsher with her then, too. I was mainly doing artist interview coaching at that stage in my career. So I wanted to help her, the female I liked. Except I didn't really help. I was far too harsh with her, not wanting to treat her as special or anything.

"She floundered in her first interview, I was no help to her at all. And from what I know she hasn't done another interview since. She hasn't spoken to me since then, either. Sebastian barely tolerates me, too. He is still cold with me when we speak now."

Hyacinth has wrapped her arms around herself, and I can see that she feels conflicted.

"I just know that Addison wants absolutely nothing to do with me. And I'm upset, because I know that once she finds out about us, she'll try to split us up."

"Oh, Liliana..." she starts, and I can see that she is going to try and come up with a solution. But I have to live with the consequences of my actions. I just didn't think that it might cost me my mate.

"Everything is done for the party. My team can look after the rest. So I think I'm just going to go home, I'm exhausted from this week."

"Let me come home with you." She cups my face in her hands, pulling me down to kiss her. I break our kiss early, though.

"It's OK, princess." I stroke her cheek. "Go have fun, enjoy the party. Make sure that Addison dances with you."

With that, I walk away to find my car.

Chapter 33

*A*ddison

I hang around with Maddox and Nereus by the bar, the party picking up tempo around me. The lights are annoying, and I would rather be at home with my little human.

Speaking of Hyacinth, I see her come back into the space. She looks uncomfortable as she eyes up the people in the room. I wave to her, and start the process of making my way through this crowd.

I saw her leaving with someone not too long ago. The glimpse that I caught looked like the tail and wing of a succubus. I know Hyacinth has been seeing someone else... but if that someone else is Liliana? Not good. She's the only succubus at the label though, so I have to hope it was just friendly.

Even so... Liliana is not someone that I want around my little human. I said as much when she first started and that bitch was assigned as her buddy. I thought Hyacinth was more astute than this, that she would see through someone like Liliana's bullshit. Everyone else Hyacinth chooses to surround herself with seems to be decent.

When I get close enough to her, I can see that there is a sadness in her eyes. She looks like she's trying to hold in tears. Her lip wobbles as she looks up at me, her chocolate brown orbs swimming.

I make a split second decision to cheer her up.

"Dance with me!" I shout over the music. She hesitantly takes my hand and lets me pull her onto the dance floor.

I spin her around, earning myself some giggles and a smile, before I pull out some of the dorkiest dance moves that I can muster. It's fun, she copies some of my moves and we fall into fits of laughter. She might be worse than me when it comes to dancing.

We last about two songs before she presses up against me. Our laughter dies out as we grind against one another, dancing like two people who have fucked each other. Her eyes meet mine, her lips pouting ever so softly.

"Do you want to go outside?" I lean down and whisper in her ear.

Instead of letting me take her, Hyacinth pulls me along and out the front door of the studio. It's hot seeing her lead me along, knowing what she wants from me.

I am tempted to dash behind a bush and have my way with her. But instead I take the lead and bring her to my car. Opening the backseat, I sit inside and pull her onto my lap, shutting the door behind her. The leather of the seat sticks to my sweat slicked skin.

"Ooh, the backseat..?" She teases, running her hands through my hair.

Instead of replying, I pull her down into a kiss. We writhe against one another, eagerly showing our devotion, hands roaming.

A wolf whistle sounds from close by. Too close. A glance at the window isn't enough, the car having already fogged up from our heavy breathing. I need to look closer. Breaking our kiss, I lean forward, trying to see out the window. Hyacinth continues her kisses, working her way down my neck.

I get close enough to the window just as Nereus' gaze meets mine. The bastard has the audacity to wave. I realize a little too belatedly that Hyacinth is still kissing my neck and grinding up on me.

"Hyacinth, babe." I grip her by the shoulders so she knows I'm being serious. "We have an audience."

"What?" She looks confused, and it strikes me that she's maybe had a bit too much to drink.

"Just give me a second." I crack the door open and already I can hear Maddox's voice. He's chastising Nereus for approaching the car. What the fuck?

I leave Hyacinth in the back seat, shutting the door behind me.

"What the fuck, dude?"

"Sorry, sorry." Nereus chuckles, lifting his hands up in surrender. "I promise, I really didn't expect you to be making out in there. This fucker was giving me a hard time and I came out to get some fresh air."

He gestures with a tentacle back at Maddox, and again I wonder if the pair are more than just friends.

"Can a girl not get some fucking peace in a parking lot?"

Nereus shrugs just as the car door opens behind me.

"Hi," Hyacinth's voice is small behind me. She sidles up to me, and I wrap an arm around her shoulder.

"Not sure if we've properly met, I'm Nereus." At least he doesn't hold out a tentacle for her to shake. I think Hyacinth might die on the spot if he did.

"I'm Hyacinth." She sounds more confident now, but she still clings to me.

Maddox finally joins us and huffs a nod in her direction.

"You guys might just want to go home. Seems like a few people are leaving the party now. You don't want to get caught by someone who doesn't already know about this."

He gestures between us.

"Oh!" Hyacinth lets out a surprised sound. Maybe she thought I hadn't told my friends about us?

I pull her to me, my lips brushing her earlobe as I speak. "How about I finally take you around to my place?"

"That's our cue," Maddox says. He half drags Nereus with him and towards his truck.

"What was that all about?" Hyacinth asks me.

"I have no fucking idea."

Chapter 34

H*yacinth*

I'm excited to see Addison's house. I feel like she would live in a really cool basement or something, she just gives me basement studio vibes.

It's certainly not what I'm picturing, that's for sure. After driving down a street filled with expensive looking townhouses, I realize that I was maybe thinking about this wrong.

Addison has produced multiple award winning albums... of course she's loaded. It's even more so than I thought. She pulls into the drive of a detached house, set nicely apart from the townhouses around it. Shit.

"I have to say that I'm embarrassed that you have seen my tiny bedroom now." I can't help but blurt.

"Stop," she switches off the engine. "I love your tiny bedroom. It's so perfectly you."

She pecks a kiss on my nose before hopping out of the car. I follow her into the house through the front door. The house has a *foyer*.

Everything is sleek and modern, and also much cleaner than I expected. Addison leads me through the foyer and into a spacious kitchen. I know she definitely doesn't use this space much, at least.

"Do you want a snack?" Addison asks me.

I thought we might be doing something a bit sexier than having a snack. But I do feel a little bit tipsy, so maybe she's right about the whole snack thing. She doesn't wait for my response, grabbing a tub of guacamole from the fridge and a bag of tortilla chips. Yum.

Hopping up onto a bar stool, I barely wait for her to open them before I dig in. A snack is exactly what I needed. I'm on my fourth chip when Addison starts to speak.

"Do you want to tell me why you were so upset earlier?"

I swallow my bite slowly, wiping my hands clean as I do. I can't help the sigh that escapes me.

"I'm still seeing someone else," I clear my throat. This is not going to be a fun conversation. "Well, that person saw us together. They were upset, but not because I was with someone else, they knew that. It was more because they saw that the person was you."

"It was Liliana, wasn't it?" She looks so disappointed in me, I can't bear it. I simply nod, my fight leaving me as she sighs, rubbing her temples. Addison takes my hand in hers, searching my eyes. The concern in her violet eyes is upsetting. I can already feel my tears welling up.

"Liliana just isn't a nice person, honey. I'm sorry you had to find out this way, but you can do so much better. And I don't mean me, even though I want it to be me... Liliana is a harsh, mean person."

I pull my hand away, standing up and pacing.

"You don't even know her!" My anger flares, she's not even trying to listen. "You had a few sour interactions with her years ago. I *know* Liliana, and she is a wonderfully kind and generous person. I think you both need to speak with each other, because there's absolutely been a misunderstanding here.

"It's not my place to broker peace between you."

There's already an argument brewing on Addison's face as I speak.

I can't stay here. I shouldn't have come back with Addison, I should have just called an Uber home when I was at the studio. Now I'm stuck on the wrong side of the city.

"I think I'd like to go home."

"I'll drive you." Addison quips, her voice blunt and harsh. She grabs the keys and gets up to leave right away.

The drive to my house is filled with a quiet tension. It's so frustrating that I needed her help to get home, too.

"Thanks for the ride," I say when we finally pull up to my house. She doesn't respond, and I just leave her there.

Chapter 35

L*iliana*

My wine sloshes in my glass, almost tipping over the edge. I pause my pacing and place it on the coffee table. The last thing I need is to spill red wine on my carpet tonight.

Did you get home OK?

I send the text to Hyacinth. I shouldn't have left her at the party to possibly make her own way home. But I also knew that I couldn't have stayed without ruining poor

Hyacinth's night. It was her first big party with the label. Fuck, I probably did ruin it for her, anyway.

Why couldn't I have just told her I was fine? I could have laughed it off and told her to go have fun. Maybe even danced with her a little.

That wouldn't have worked though. Hyacinth knows me so well at this stage. She saw right through me.

I'm not really sure how to move on from here. I know that Hyacinth is mine, and I won't let her go. But I don't know how I'm going to navigate her dating Addison too.

God... why did it have to be Addison?

I was into her when she first joined the label. But I thought she was far too cool for me. She would have been so much better off without any coaching from me at all. She would have pulled off that aloof attitude in interviews so well.

I just had to get in my head about it, didn't I? I thought that if I was harder on her, that I could help her. That was long before I learned any kind of nuance. Not that I'm much better these days, either.

After I fucked up her training, I knew I had no chance. So I just blocked her out. I tried my best not to think about her in that way, to shut down my attraction.

Had I been wrong to do that?

Addison really has grown into herself. Maybe not in the PR sense, but in every other way. She's a powerhouse. And if I'm being honest, I don't think Sebastian would be anywhere near as successful without her input. She's come a long way, her success outweighing anything I've ever done.

And now that I'm allowing my thoughts to stray there, she is absolutely breathtaking. Her violet hair, the silky strands look so soft to the touch. I imagine what it would be like to run my fingers through them. Those intelligent eyes that match her perfectly. Her grumpy demeanor. It was a mistake to let her slip between my fingers the first time.

She's not actually our third mate, is she?

Surely, I would have known that by now.

But, what if she is? Fuck, I've been such a fool. If Addison is my mate then I have been the absolute worst alpha to her. Poor Addison, she would have been so much more vulnerable with me as her alpha all those years ago. It's an instinctual response, she might not have even been aware of it.

My comments, my behavior, it would have crushed her. I destroyed her with my disregard and then my ignorance over the past few years. God, how badly had I fucked this up?

I down the rest of my wine. This is going to take a lot of damage control.

Checking my phone, I see a reply from Hyacinth to say that she got home safe. It's accompanied by a photo of her frog tucked under a leaf. She is so adorable.

Chapter 36

A*ddison*

My hands are laden with coffee and donuts, the key to anyone's heart. Although, instead of going to Hyacinth's to grovel this morning, I'm heading to Sebastian's.

He called me last night to tell me the news that he and Flora have officially mated. I can't believe it! I know they had been spending a lot of time together, and they released the song—yes, I'm still a tad annoyed about that—but I didn't realize they were ready to mate. I didn't realize they really were mates, either. Sebastian had never mentioned it to me or the guys. Although, I'm not one to talk, I haven't properly spoken to him about my thoughts on Hyacinth.

I'm happy for him though, truly. Flora has brightened him up and softened his edges. I think he needed that. I'm so happy for them. And yet, it does make me jealous. I want to have that with Hyacinth.

I'm doing a shitty job of fixing things with her though. I didn't even try last night when I should have. It was late, and I wanted her to see that she was wrong about Liliana. Now that I've had a bit of space, I realize that maybe I was too harsh. Harsh with Hyacinth, at least.

I just need to get Liliana out of the picture. Then maybe I will be able to mate Hyacinth properly, too. Something about that just doesn't feel right though. Getting rid of Liliana sounds like it would solve all of my problems, but the thought just feels so wrong. Deep in my core, I know that's not the right thing to do.

My house is a ten minute walk to Sebastian's, with a convenient coffee shop in between. It's why we used to never go into the Fortune Records studio, if we could help it. We both had pretty good home studio set ups, and I preferred producing at home. Maybe if Flora moves in with Sebastian we can go back to doing that. Hyacinth could stay with me sometimes and Flora could use one of our home studios to record...

I shake my head, Hyacinth is currently not speaking to me. I need to fix things with her before I start daydreaming about those kinds of things.

Shuffling the things in my hand, I ring the bell at Sebastian's front door.

"Addison! How are you?" Flora exclaims, opening the door and going in for a hug. She pauses when she sees the coffee and takeout bag. "Ooh, you brought treats! You are the absolute best. Come on in."

She takes the coffee from me and steps aside to let me past. "Congratulations, Flora. You must be so excited. I'm thrilled for you both."

Flora blushes slightly, her joy written all over her face. Her mating mark is on full display in her sundress. I'm a little jealous, if I'm being honest. I want to be claimed like that, too.

"I was thinking we could sit out on the roof." I follow her up the staircase.

Sebastian's house has the prettiest rooftop terrace. A definite must for a dragon shifter, he can easily take off and land from there when he's in his dragon form. I wonder what Flora thinks of him in that form. Probably good things, if she decided to complete their bond.

We sit at the cute dining set, one of the only feminine touches Sebastian really has at his house. That was all going to change though, I can imagine.

"I really am so excited for you, Flora." She really is beautiful, her golden hair gleaming in the sun. I envy her tan complexion, I would get so sunburnt with a dragon shifter mate. They're obsessed with perching on high points on sunny days.

"I have to admit that I've been so awful with trying to get to know you better." I continue.

"Are you for real? I'm totally the worst! I've been so standoffish." She flicks her hair over a shoulder. "Either way, I'm excited you're here now. I want to hear everything about you."

I laugh a little awkwardly. "I'm not sure that there's too much to tell..."

"Well," her golden eyes gleam with mischief. "How's *your* love life?"

I can tell by that look that she knows exactly what she's doing. I'm almost certain that Hyacinth let something slip, especially with Alex around. But Flora seems pretty genuine, maybe she can help with my Liliana problem.

"It's a tad more dramatic after last night, to tell the truth."

"Oh?" She patiently waits for me to fill in the silence. And boy do I. Spilling the beans on everything, I give her the back story with Liliana and catch her up on Hyacinth and then the events of last night. Flora gives me the space to let it all out. I don't think I realized how much I needed to tell someone.

"So, you're sure Hyacinth is your mate?" She asks me when I eventually finish. Our donuts are long gone, the ice cubes in our coffees melted away.

"All the signs are there," I slurp at the end of my drink, trying to get that last drop. But my paper straw has long since disintegrated. "But I know that she's mine, in my gut, I know that. There's also just this niggling part of me that is telling me that something is missing too."

"Maybe you have another mate, then." The deep and gravelly voice of Sebastian pipes in as he pulls up a chair next to us. How long has he been standing there, listening in? Fucking shifters and their creepy silent walking.

At least he's a good distraction. I let out a squeal, jumping up and tackling him into a hug. I tend to forget how enormous he is until I'm hugging him.

"Congratulations on your mating, Seb!" He actually cracks a decently big smile for him. "Tell me about it, it's a way better topic than my problems. What are your plans? Are you having a party?"

I look to Flora, thinking that the mention of a party would be distraction enough. She and Sebastian share a look though, and I know I'm deep in shit. Her eyes soften as she looks back to me. Six feet of shit.

"Maybe you need to meet up with Liliana. Clear the air, you know? I found her a bit harsh when I met her, but she was just doing her job. I think her whole stick is that she tries to prep you for the worst interview possible.

"Maybe you should try to understand her perspective a little."

Why does every-fucking-thing lead back to Liliana?

"Also, it would be good if you didn't involve Hyacinth in that. Just make it about you two." Flora adds, ripping away my safety net.

"It's a good idea," Sebastian agrees. "And you know I'm not Liliana's biggest fan."

They relax in their seats while I process things. If I'm being real with myself, it did sound pretty stupid when I was saying it out loud. The reason that I got mad at Liliana all those years ago. Maybe in her own twisted way she was trying to help me.

That didn't stop her from completely ignoring me for years after, though.

Has she really been my mate this whole time? I highly doubt it. But if I need to be on good terms with her to make Hyacinth happy, then I guess I'm open to it.

"Fine," I give in. "I'll reach out to Liliana. But I can't help it if she doesn't want to fix things on her end."

Chapter 37

Liliana

My third cup of coffee is steaming and I follow the marbling wisps with my gaze. I sometimes find focusing on steam or fire while I'm trying to think through a problem helps me.

My phone dings with the chime I've set for Hyacinth's contact. I quickly grab it, my meditation forgotten. We haven't spoken since the night of the party. Every time I pick up my phone to reach out to her, my shame stops me.

Hey, sorry I haven't reached out. I've just needed some alone time. I have the week off work so I was thinking it might be good to have some space for that time. I also was kinda hoping that you and Addison might reach out to each other. Maybe you have already. Anyway, sorry this is so long I just wanted to explain myself. You two should talk though if you haven't—and I wanna give you space to do that.

She quickly follows up with another text that has Addison's phone number.

Fuck.

I should have already reached out to Addison myself. There's no excuse, I have everyone at the studio's number.

I should be with Hyacinth, looking after my little omega. There's only one thing I can do now, I need to try and rectify things with Addison. Especially if it turns out that she is our mate, too. Honestly, what do I think I'm doing? Do I think I'm just going to know whether or not she's our mate without actually reaching out to her? Without seeing her?

Swallowing my pride, I type out a text to Addison.

Chapter 38

I stare at my phone again. If I keep staring at it the message might delete itself into oblivion. Fingers crossed.

I've been bored out of my mind the past couple days. When I started to consider going home to my parents for a visit, I knew something was definitely wrong. Sebastian was taking the week off to spend time with Flora and help her move in with him. I would have offered with the whole moving thing, but Maddox had them covered.

God, what did I even do with my time before I started seeing Hyacinth?

Picking up the annoying piece of tech, I head to my living room to watch some TV. Except I don't look at the screen at all. I'm still staring at this fucking phone sitting on my coffee table.

Hyacinth texted me yesterday, asking for some space for the week. Her one request? Meet up with Liliana to talk things out.

I know I said I would chat to her when I was with Flora and Sebastian. But saying that and putting it into practice are two very different things.

Of course Liliana texted me pretty much straight after Hyacinth. Instead of replying, I've been staring at my phone like it's going to kill me for the past day.

Picking up my phone again, I open up the chat with Liliana.

Can we meet up and talk? Liliana x

What was with the little 'x' anyway? I know I'm going to have to reply sooner or later. If Hyacinth reaches out and finds out that I've been sitting on this? I don't want her to be disappointed in me.

Yes we can meet—coffee tomorrow?

I've barely set my phone back down when it buzzes with a response. That was quick.

No. I'm taking you out to lunch. What's your address? I will pick you up.

Typical Liliana, trying to take control of everything. A typical alpha move too, making the whole meeting on her terms. Whatever, I just need to get this over with. I text her back to say it's fine and give her the details.

Liliana

For the first time in years, I am seriously questioning myself. I've tried on six different outfits, at least.

Hyacinth says that I can come across as intimidating, even when I don't mean to. And I certainly don't want to turn off Addison today. Perhaps a softer look is what I need.

I pull out a silk dress I hardly wear, its slippery material is along the lines of what I'm going for. The color is a deep gray with a metallic sheen that compliments my skin tone well. I button up the dress and then slip on a designer belt to cinch my waist.

The drive to her place is ridiculously quick. Have we been this close to each other the whole time? Not even just in work, but the fact that we live so close is unbelievable.

I'm not surprised when I see her luxurious home. She's been a successful producer for years now, I'm sure she easily out-earns me. I leave the engine running, once I pull up her drive.

It doesn't take long for Addison to come out to meet me.

She looks adorable in a lavender sundress that ends at her knees. Blues and purples always look so good on her. Her hair is swept up into a high ponytail, and I'm grateful for the unobstructed view of her pretty face.

"Hi," she sounds a bit nervous as she situates herself in the seat. "I wasn't sure what to wear."

Addison tugs on the hem of her dress to stop it from riding up.

"You look perfect." I start to drive us to the restaurant. "I had no idea what to wear either."

"Really?" She scoffs. "I didn't think you were ever unsure of anything."

"Then you may have misunderstood me, Addison." A wonderful aroma fills the car. Violets, smoke, and a hint of petrichor. It's a fitting scent for an electro witch, that's for sure. Why is it only now that I am finally noticing it?

I picked a pretty nice place for lunch. It's an upscale French restaurant, some place that could feel like a date if you wanted, but also casual enough. We're seated quickly and I order us some water for the table.

It's the first time in a while that I haven't been somewhere demon run. I've been careful with Hyacinth around, but that's not a worry with Addison.

"So..." Addison awkwardly tries to say something, and comes up short.

If I actually am her alpha, then I need to start making her feel comfortable with me.

"I know with the timing of everything, it might have seemed like I only set this up because of Hyacinth's text. But I was meaning to reach out, after the party."

"Me too, actually." She replies.

The waiter takes our orders and we're finally left to ourselves again.

"I want to apologize, Addison." She looks shocked. This is clearly not what she thought I was going to say. "I thought you were so beautiful, and so intelligent when we first met. I could tell that you had the talent and the drive to be successful.

"But I was also attracted to you." Her eyes widen even further at my admission. "I had never had any sort of attraction with anyone at work before. So I didn't know how to handle it. In the end, I treated you so poorly. I thought that if I was too nice, it would be because I liked you, and it wouldn't do anything to help you."

She's silent, her mouth slightly open as she processes everything I've said.

"I realize now that I was young and stupid. I made a mistake, Addison, and I'm sorry that it took me this long to realize it."

"That interview destroyed me," Addison's eyes well up with tears. "I stopped after that, let Sebastian take the limelight."

"I am so sorry that was because of me."

"It wasn't just you," she sniffles. "It was me too. I would've tanked the interview anyway, even if you had been good at coaching me. I think at the time I just didn't want to admit that it was me who fucked up. It was much easier to blame it on you."

Something settles in me at her admission. What I did was wrong, but she doesn't really blame me. I was just a convenient scapegoat.

"Thank you for saying that." I gently brush my knee against hers under the table.

Chapter 39

*A*ddison

This lunch is going much better than I expected. Even if I did sort of cry a little.

I can't believe that she had a thing for me. An actual *succubus*, a fucking hot one at that, was attracted to me when I was a fresh baby in the music industry. I remember how intimidated I was by her. No wonder some harsh words went straight through me.

But it was years ago, and we've both grown up a lot since then.

Liliana looks so beautiful today, too, that it makes it hard to even consider being upset with her. The soft lines of her dress contrast with her striking features. I could get lost in those piercing red eyes as well. Her wings are tucked neatly around the back of her chair. I can't help but notice them as she moves and speaks, the way they twitch when she's a bit nervous or hesitant to say something.

I can imagine her with Hyacinth, how they would look together. I feel like she's already picked up a few of her mannerisms. That thought doesn't annoy me in the way that I thought it would.

It's nice that Liliana took me to such a nice place for lunch. She insisted on paying when the bill came. It feels nice to be looked after, maybe I don't *hate* how she takes control with things.

"Can I take you out to dinner tomorrow night?"

Her question takes me by surprise. She wants to see me again? I thought this was just about us making things amicable for Hyacinth's sake.

"As a date." Liliana clarifies. "If you're interested, that is."

The way she says it with such a suggestive tone makes my toes curl. I hesitate though, do I want to go on a date with Liliana?

"Don't worry, you don't have to answer me now." She signs the check with a flourish, slipping her card back into her purse. "Text me if you decide you want to go. I will have the table booked anyway."

Chapter 40

Hyacinth

I curl up in my bed, huddled under the sheets with my handheld gaming console. This is the only activity that doesn't bore me to tears at the moment, but God knows how long that will last.

My room is lit by the console and Alfred's vivarium. His little frog noises the only sound.

The house has been empty apart from me. Both Sam and Riley went home to their families this week. I never thought I would say this, but I could really do with having to go into work right now. Maybe I should have visited my parents this week too.

The urge to text Addison and Liliana to check in has been so tempting. Every time I have to remind myself that they need their space to sort things out. That's if things *can* be sorted.

Liliana had seemed so defeated, and Addison so closed off to the idea. I just hope that they have at least met up and tried at this point.

It's only been a couple days, but my chest aches from missing them both. I'm miserable, my room not even bringing me its usual solace.

My life has been a whirlwind since I started my new job and met my females. I feel so changed by it all in a very permanent way. It's wild to me that only a few weeks ago, I was going on dates with men and I had no idea about my queerness.

That's one thing I can be happy about at least. While I don't recognize the girl I was a few weeks ago anymore, I've never felt more like myself.

I really hope that Addison and Liliana work things out. I can't imagine my life without either of them anymore. They're both so important to me in their own way.

I turn back over, switching off my console and trying to sleep some more.

Chapter 41

Addison

I caved on the dinner date pretty quickly. It didn't even end up being a text. By the time Liliana dropped me at my house I told her I would go.

Am I still coming to terms with everything? Yes. But I also can't ignore the undeniable attraction between us. What does that mean for me? I have no idea.

Knowing Liliana's taste, it's surely a nice restaurant that she will be taking me to, tonight. So I went all out with getting ready.

It was difficult to get into my corset on my own, but I managed. It's a rich black satin, and I've layered it over a deep purple pleated skirt. The look emphasizes my curves, pushing my boobs up nicely. I wear my layered crystal necklaces, as usual. The whole outfit is tied together with my heeled lace-up booties.

I know I look pretty good, but I can't help but feel nervous for tonight. If you had asked me yesterday morning, this is the last thing that I would be doing. Liliana was so kind though, so understanding, and she gave the perfect apology.

Both of our initial responses to one another was attraction. I think that's worth exploring again. I put the last few items in my purse just in time, the sound of an engine pulling into my drive.

I'm surprised when I leave the house to see a sleek black car that is definitely not what Liliana drove yesterday. It is Liliana that gets out of the back seat though, holding the door for me to get in.

"Hey, Liliana." I say, pausing as we stand close. I'm not sure if I should hug her in greeting, or just get in the car.

Liliana leans forward, completely in my personal space. The tension is tangible, and I have to reign in the electricity itching to escape from the surface of my skin.

"Hello, little witch." Her lips almost brush my ear as she speaks. I feel a tremor straight through to my pussy. Fuck.

I can feel the temperature in my body go up a notch, a flush forming on my neck and chest.

"Spin for me." I blink, trying to catch up with myself. What?

One look in her crimson eyes and I can see that she's dead serious. Fuck it, she really just wants to see my outfit from all angles.

I take a step away and give her a twirl.

"Positively delicious," her smile shows a glimpse of fang. I need to be bitten by those sexy fangs.

I clear my throat and get into the car. Liliana is wearing one of her sleek fitting suits, tonight in a burgundy shade. There is nothing under her blazer, and I can see the outline of her cleavage when she leans forward.

"I want us to treat tonight as a fresh start." She begins, sliding into the seat next to me. "Obviously we don't need to pretend not to know each other. But let's try not to focus on our past. What do you think?"

I think that I would agree to a lot of things with her bent over me like this. The intensity of her gaze, her alpha presence, those exquisite horns... they make me want to obey. I'm a light switch, in general. I can top with Hyacinth when we need, but I much prefer to be utterly possessed. Liliana is looking at me like she wants to possess me.

"Addison," She tucks my hair away from my face. "Use your words."

"Y-yes," I clear my throat. "Fresh start. Got it."

The car journey to the restaurant is short but intense. Liliana stays turned towards me, giving me her full attention as we chat. She doesn't speak in such a suggestive tone again, but the way she looks at me makes me want to skip dinner and jump her in this car.

She explains that she hired a car for the evening so that we could both drink if we wanted to.

The restaurant that she takes me to is one I've heard of a few times now. It's a very exclusive sushi house run by a pretty famous chef, as far as I am aware. Who did she know to get a booking here so quickly?

"Perks of the PR job." She provides, obviously seeing my face.

We're seated quickly in the main room. It's noisy, but I can still hear Liliana as she speaks. She asks me about my family, and what I do outside of work.

Once I get comfortable, I start running my mouth. Complaining tends to be one of my favorite pastimes. She listens intently, laughing at the right moments, and commiserating when she should too. It's really nice to be heard by someone who gets what it's like to be a working female in this world.

She explains to me about how stressful that launch party was. How much of a nuisance Ivy was too, and that she is hoping to take some time off soon.

At some point during dessert, the mood shifts slightly. Liliana's conversation isn't quite so friendly, there's an intense sexual energy about her. Her horns glisten in the candlelight, her wings flaring as much as they can in the space.

Liliana's tail brushes against my leg, her gaze fixed on mine. I have to focus to properly swallow the sip of wine I just drank. I can't tell if the slight buzz I am feeling is from the alcohol, or if it's some magic that Liliana is working on me. I belatedly remember that Liliana is not just any demon, she's a succubus. If I let this go where I think this is going...

"Do you want to get out of here?" She asks, her tail wrapped fully around my calf now. I wonder what that feels like wrapped around other parts of me.

"Yes." I lick my lips, a flutter beginning in my lower abdomen.

Liliana signals the waiter, paying our bill quickly and leaving what appears to be a very generous tip.

Her tail releases me so that I can stand up from my seat. But when we start to walk, her hand is pressed to my lower back, her wing stretched protectively around me. It feels so good to have her physically display an interest in me like this, in front of a restaurant filled with people.

She texts the driver while we are walking and he is pulling up by the time we are properly out on the street. Ever the gentlewoman, Liliana holds the door to the car open for me again.

"I'd like to go back to your place." I tell her, mustering up all the confidence I have as she sits next to me.

"God, I thought you'd never fucking ask." Liliana pulls me onto her lap, and my legs fall on either side of her. She's so beautiful up close like this, her eyes glowing ever so softly in the dim light. There are flecks of copper, crimson, magenta... I had no idea how stunning they were up close.

My hands cup her face, and I gently press my lips to hers. She tastes like red currants and cinnamon laced with caramel, sinfully decadent. I let out a moan at the flavor, licking her lips to gain entrance and taste more.

Liliana's hands tighten on my ass as she lets me explore her mouth. Her hands having already explored under my skirt, my tiny thong leaving my cheeks bare for her.

Clearly done with my gentle exploring, Liliana takes control of the kiss. My hand wanders and strokes her black tipped ear and the groan she sounds at the touch makes my pussy gush. I've never responded on this sort of base level with an alpha before. Cum is starting to leak out of my panties by the time the car pulls up at her building.

I slip off her lap so that we can get out of the car. I have barely followed her out when she scoops me up into her arms, bridal style. I'm so turned on by how easily she can lift me.

"I can't have you dripping everywhere on the way up to the apartment." She teases and I bury my head in her neck.

I swear she has the ability to speed up time, because we are inside her apartment door and she is setting me back on the floor in a blink. She flips us so that my back is pressed against the exit, caging me in with her wings.

"Safe words?" She asks me, hands pressed on either side of my head. We're both breathing heavily with the effort to hold ourselves back.

"Lemon to slow, pineapple to stop."

"That's a good little witch." My heart stops as she kisses between my boobs right where they are pushed up by my corset.

"I think you might have made a mess down here." Her hand grazes my thigh, teasing the edge of my skirt.

"Do you need me to clean it up?"

"Yes, mommy." I bite my lip, nodding softly.

"Fuck," she drops to her knees before me, pushing my skirt up and getting a good look at me. "Call me mommy again."

"Can you please clean me up, mommy?"

I hear a tearing sound as my panties fall to the floor. Liliana buries her head between my legs, her tongue lapping at my clit. Pleasure erupts through my core and I grip her horns to stay steady.

Holy shit, I think her tongue is shifting against me. The base of her tongue stays pressed to my clit, while the tip lengthens and enters my pussy. I see stars when it all starts to vibrate.

"Yes," I moan, gripping harder on her horns.

I don't think I'm going to last that long like this. But I do know that horns are sensitive, I send a current through my fingers and Liliana buckles against me in shock. Her vibrations increase and I keep the current of electricity pulsing between her horns.

My pleasure crests and I peak, a high pitched sound escaping me.

Liliana stands, wrapping my legs around her waist and lifting me. I'm carried into a plush bedroom and deposited on even softer blankets.

"That was a neat trick," Liliana smirks at me from above, her glorious wings on full display.

"I could say the same to you."

Her tail creeps up my leg and torso, pausing at my chest and then curling around my neck. She doesn't add much pressure, just enough to let me know she's there. It feels so comforting, being wrapped in Liliana's embrace.

"I may have made this mess worse." She clucks her tongue at me. "I think I'm going to need to get you out of these clothes and get a good look at what we're dealing with here."

Her tail loosens slightly and she grips my hips, flipping me onto my front in an easy move. My arms splay in front of me and I just relax into the feeling. Oh, it feels so good to submit to her like this. Liliana slowly unhooks my corset, one rung at a time. She leaves a trail of kisses in her wake, her tail putting pressure back on my neck.

I am a whimpering mess by the time she reaches the last clasp. Her arm brackets my waist as she flips me back around, removing the corset from under me at the same time. She licks her lips before she attacks my boobs with her mouth.

All I can do is fist her hair and horns, relaxing into the pleasure she is racking upon me.

"Can I use my powers on you, little witch?"

"Fuck, yes." I groan as a new type of pleasure fills me. My nerve endings have never felt like this before. Every graze, every minuscule touch lights a fire in me. It's all so much, and yet not enough. Almost as if she can control when and how I climax. I've never been under this much control before and I never want it to stop.

Liliana's tail lifts me into a seated position by my neck as she stands over me. I stay in place as she removes her tail and strips for me. She is slim and muscled, her taut body so beautiful. I want to reach out and touch her but I don't want to make a wrong move either.

"Be a good girl and lick mommy's pussy."

Oh my god, when she speaks to me like that... I sit forward, gripping her legs and breathing her in. My tongue darts out and she tastes even better here. The crisp currant taste makes me melt. Not to mention the pleasure that is still consuming me from her powers. I trace little circles around her clit with my tongue until she is crying out with the most delicious sound.

I feel my own pleasure building, but she doesn't let me cum just yet. So I keep working her pussy, sliding two fingers inside her easily. I thrust up and in, creating friction in the best places for her.

She tightens her tail enough to cut off my breath when she orgasms this time. I'm writhing in my spot, the sheets drenched beneath me when she finally lets me cum. I'm lightheaded from both the pleasure and the lack of air.

When she releases her hold, I cum again, my pussy clenching around nothing in the most exquisite torture.

Chapter 42

L*iliana*

Addison is curled up into my side, her head smushed into my boob as she snores softly. She looks so peaceful and innocent like this, devoid of her usual frown.

Last night was magnificent. Her scent wafts over me in a blanket of violets, and I know that she is my mate. Surely she must feel it, too?

Things have moved much quicker than I anticipated, and I don't want to push her too soon. My omegas are my priority, and I will give them both whatever space they need.

It was precious to have my time alone with Addison last night, but I can't help imagining how all three of us would come together. I've never felt more happy, knowing that is a possibility.

I need to be extra careful with Addison over the next few days. I need to be prepared if she goes into heat. Hyacinth may not experience a heat at all, so I am less worried about her right now.

Addison's indigo lashes blink up at me, her violet eyes shining even in the dimness of the room.

"G'morning." She slurs through her words, blinking her eyes some more.

"Are you a grumpy girl in the mornings?" I tease, stroking her hair tenderly.

She huffs in agreement, snuggling back into me. It's adorable.

I gently extricate myself from her arms. When she protests, I tell her that coffee is coming up. That earns me a reprieve.

"Sugar." She croaks out after me.

OK, good to know. I make up a tray with sugar and milk so she can make it to her liking and bring the coffees back into the room.

"Is the grumpy witch awake?"

She grumbles something and moves to a seated position.

"Time is it?" she asks as I set the tray down next to her.

"It's 10am," I gently brush the hair back from her face and behind her ear. "Why? Do you need to be somewhere today?"

She nods her head, yawning and rubbing at her eyes. She makes her coffee and I take a mental note of her method.

"I need to go to Sebastian's for the mating party later." She nods to herself, as if she's making a to do list for just her.

"Of course," I kiss her forehead. "I'll drive you back to your house in plenty of time to get ready."

"Thank you." She looks up at me with the most open and vulnerable expression. Almost as if there is something she wants to say.

"Should we talk about Hyacinth?" Addison asks.

"Yes, that's a good idea." I run a hand through my unruly morning hair. "I don't know how either of you will feel about this, but I want both of you. Together, separately, both."

Addison pauses with the coffee cup half way to her mouth.

"I think I might like that, too."

I nod, thinking about how we might bring this up with Hyacinth.

"It could be cute if we go over to Hyacinth's place together tomorrow." Addison suggests. "We could bring it up with her then somehow."

That's a great idea.

We work on our plan right up until I need to bring Addison home. I hope she might bring me to events like this soon enough.

Chapter 43

*H*yacinth

My week of space is up today. I decide not to immediately text either Liliana or Addison. Let them come to me, save myself some embarrassment. I have probably pushed them both away with this space.

I twist and turn in my bed, the place I have spent at least 85% of this week. This time alone has been depressing, to say the least. I feel like I have lost all hope in everything good.

Will they have actually met up with one another? Or will they have seen my request as annoying and decided it was much easier to let me go than deal with this?

A soft knock sounds on my door. Riley and Samantha were both due in late last night, but I haven't seen either of them yet. I sigh, no one needs to see me in this state.

The door cracks open and Riley steps into the room.

"Hey, babe. Someone is here to see you."

What? Who would be here to see me? Unless... it could be one of my females.

Oh no. While I would be so happy to see either of them, I look like a hot mess. I hop out of my bed to look at myself. The last time I showered was three days ago and I had horrible bags under my eyes from crying and lack of sleep. I smoosh down my hair, trying to make my curls look presentable. It doesn't do anything.

I guess this is what I am going to look like.

Riley walks down the stairs ahead of me, his eyes filled with worry. I'm nervous anyway, and that doesn't make me feel any better. What does he know that I don't?

Following him into the kitchen, I'm taken aback by the sight before me.

Both Addison and Liliana are here. In my house. They wear matching hopeful expressions that make me so happy and confused all at once. This must be good news, right? They wouldn't show up together to break up with me.

Addison moves to me first, holding out a bouquet of fluffy purple flowers.

"They're Asters," She says, "I checked and they're safe to be around Alfred."

Tears well up in my eyes at her thoughtfulness.

"I'm sorry for not hearing you out sooner, for not listening to you about Liliana. She's great, and I needed to give her a chance."

She wipes away my tears and sets the flowers down on the kitchen counter. Liliana joins us now. Strangely, she sniffs at the air.

"My Dad was definitely right," she announces. "Can we chat somewhere private? I need to speak to you both about something."

It's a strange thing for her to say, but her face is so serious that I take them up to my room right away.

Chapter 44

L*iliana*

I'm fixated on my mates.

My *mates*.

"Do you smell it?" I turn and ask Addison.

She nods, awe on her face. Hyacinth looks between us with confusion.

"What's happening?" She asks. "What happened this week? I'm presuming you made up?"

Oh how I missed her beautiful face. Her curls are a wild and frizzy mess and the chaos suits her. I try to take my time explaining to her what has happened.

"Addison and I met for lunch initially, where we talked through our problems. It worked quite well, and we both realized that there was an attraction there. I took Addison out on a date and we had sex."

I give her a brief moment to catch up. Her face shows nothing, almost as if she knows I'm not done.

"That went well," I share a smirk with Addison. "We wanted to speak with you about how we move forward now."

"We want to see you and each other, all at once." Addison adds.

I finally take a moment to look around Hyacinth's room, all her quirky details. It is fascinating to be in her space like this. I don't know why I haven't made an effort to come up when I have been to the house.

"But we need you to pack a bag." I continue. "We need to leave here soon. We'll explain everything in the car."

Hyacinth hesitantly looks between us, the silence stretching out while we waste precious time that we don't have. I take her hands in mine.

"Do you remember our first date, when I told you all about mating and alphas and omegas?"

"Yeah, but..." Hyacinth tries to argue, but we don't have time.

"Addison and I have both just scented that we are all mates. The three of us. Which means that Addison is going to go into heat, and we need to get her somewhere safe and help her through it."

"Hyacinth can go into heat, too." Addison pipes up. "Flora went into heat with Sebastian."

"Fuck." This is worse than I thought. Hyacinth is even more vulnerable than Addison. The need to protect them both is overwhelming. "We need to get you both somewhere safe, quickly. Addison, your house is closer than mine, is that OK with you?"

"Yes, I have a nest." Perfect.

Addison finds a backpack on the floor and starts to move about Hyacinth's room, packing up things for her quickly.

"Will we be gone long?" Hyacinth is crying again, I don't think she understands what is happening. "I don't want to leave Alfred."

"We'll be a few days, at least." I tell her. "Addison, why don't you go ask Riley to look after Alfred while I help Hyacinth with the rest of her things?"

Addison kisses me on her way out, and I can see Hyacinth's eyes widen as she watches.

"I promise we will explain more in the car. We just need to get on the road, princess. OK?"

She wipes her tears away and sniffles.

"Yeah, OK. Here, let me pack that." I watch her swallow down her fear and trust me. I am so proud of her. "What do I need?"

We pack her things quickly and by the time we get downstairs, Addison has already confirmed with Riley that Alfred will be well taken care of.

Addison must have warned Riley that I might be testy, because he keeps his distance from me and Hyacinth as we head out the door.

I drove Addison here, so we have my car to take back. Which is good, I wouldn't want Addison driving in case anything happens.

Once we're on the road, we explain what going into heat means. Addison and Hyacinth sit in the back seat, Addison soothing our little human.

"Why are you both so panicked about a lot of sex?"

"It's not just the sex, sweetie." Addison replies. "We will all have our own biological response. Omegas are vulnerable when they are in heat, which sends alphas into overdrive. They need to please us, yes. But they also have a deep and primal urge to protect. That's why Liliana is so stressed right now. Her instincts are telling her that she needs to get us to safety, to a nest."

Chapter 45

***A**ddison*

I'm stressed out too by the time we get to my house. I know that's supposed to be all alpha, but I feel the need to protect my little human.

Everything changed in a matter of minutes. We were going to explain to Hyacinth in a much softer way that we had slept together. We were planning on taking her out to a nice lunch that we had booked, and then we were going to take her back to Liliana's.

Obviously, that didn't happen.

Liliana is dialing the Chinese takeout place as we walk up the drive. It sounds like she's ordering enough food to feed twenty people. But I appreciate that she's just trying to provide. We can put most of it in the fridge to last us for the next couple days. It's smart.

"I thought we were all stressed out." Hyacinth tugs on my sleeve. "Why are we ordering Chinese food now?"

"She's just trying to stock up the house and prepare us. It's the easiest way to do that right now."

"I kind of like it," she blushes. "When Liliana takes control and looks after us like that."

"Me too." We share a giggle.

I let us into the house, and we head into the living space. I set Hyacinth's bag on the floor and get to work with Liliana on prepping the house. Poor Hyacinth just stands there awkwardly as we move about.

I'll be sure to give her lots of attention in a minute, we just have to get through this. My basement is well stocked for this particular scenario. Every omega has a nest set up for when they go into heat.

I think things through for a second and change gears. I pick up Hyacinth's bag again and lead her to my bathroom. Turning the water on, I help her out of her clothes and into the shower.

"Take your time, baby. The food is on the way and you can have a nice meal with us when you're done." I kiss her on the lips quickly. "Bring down your bag with you when you're finished."

Liliana and I finish setting up the nest just as a freshly washed Hyacinth tentatively enters the living space.

The doorbell rings and we leave Liliana to it. She plates up food for both of us and we all sit around to eat. The further we get into our meal, the more relaxed Hyacinth becomes. She's slowly catching up with herself and processing everything.

When we're finished eating, Liliana cleans up and we all snuggle on the couch. I put on a trashy reality TV show and Hyacinth excitedly tells me that this is the one her and Liliana watch together.

I really didn't peg Liliana as the reality TV type.

Hyacinth and I snuggle into Liliana from either side and she tucks her wings around us both.

I've never felt more relaxed, more at peace. Even with the threat of a looming heat.

Chapter 46

Liliana

Hyacinth's scent shifts, the clementine sweetening with a peachy undertone. That's the first sign.

Both my mates are curled up against me on the couch. The TV show has been playing but none of us have really been watching it. It's been so comforting to sit like this, that we all dozed in and out of sleep.

I nudge Addison now to get her to wake up. Glancing down pointedly at Hyacinth, I whisper.

"Do you smell it?"

Addison nods, understanding on her face. She stands up, brushing herself off.

"How are you feeling?" I ask her.

"I'm good, actually. No signs from me just yet, but I'm sure it won't be long." She nods towards the door. "Come on, let's get her settled in the nest."

Hyacinth chooses that moment to stir, her brown eyes blinking up at me.

"I feel weird." Her omega whine triggers something deep inside me. Instead of doing the sensible thing and moving us downstairs, I don't stop Hyacinth as she crawls into my lap. She straddles me, gyrating against me, as her hair cascades around her. She moans and whimpers, I'm not even sure that she's aware of what she's doing.

"Do you need me to help you out, princess?"

"Mhmm," she hums in agreement, her hands moving up to cup her boobs.

Hyacinth

I feel so hot, but also really good at the same time and I have this insatiable *urge*. I don't understand though, what it is that I need.

There's a whining sound that confuses me, until I realize that it's coming from me. A hot pleasure comes from my nipples, and I look down to see that I'm playing with them through my t-shirt.

Warm hands are on my waist, but they feel good despite their heat. I look down and notice their gray-ish complexion. I make the connection that it's Liliana.

A glance up and I see her shock of red hair, a little blurry in my haze. My back arches as a new wave of pleasure breaks through me. A body catches me with theirs, careful to stop me from falling. They feel so soft and good against my back. Their arms reach around and move my hands aside, replacing them with their own. That feels even better.

"Come on, princess." The words come from in front of me. "Let's get you to the nest. It's safe and cozy."

Mhmm, that sounds nice. I barely notice being lifted, but I do register the room blurring around me and shifting as we move.

Chapter 47

*A*ddison

Liliana pulls Hyacinth forward so that she's resting on her chest. She stands up, cradling our little human against her. Poor Hyacinth is completely lost to her lust at the moment, writhing against Liliana as we make our way down to the basement.

My nest is built into the floor. There is a mattress somewhere in there, buried beneath the piles of soft throw blankets and pillows. I've even brought one of Hyacinth's favorite squish plushies from her house for her.

Liliana places her down in the nest in a seated position. I lift her arms above her head as Liliana lifts up Hyacinth's t-shirt. She's completely naked underneath, apart from her panties. Her curls are loose and flow down her back in a beautiful cascade.

We lay her on her back in the bed and I scoot in behind her, playing with her nipples. Liliana takes the opportunity to strip herself of her clothes too.

She cuts such an imposing figure, standing before us, completely naked and wings splayed. The sight makes me want to get on my knees and service her.

Hyacinth is whimpering in my arms, and I can tell that she needs *more*. I charge a gentle current, it spreads over her boobs, giving her a tingling sensation everywhere at once. She cries out at the sensation, her back arching against me.

Liliana stalks towards us, kneeling in between Hyacinth's legs. She rubs the tip of her tail in the pool of cum that is forming under Hyacinth's pussy. But instead of fucking her with it like I expect, she raises her tail to my mouth.

"Have a taste," she purrs.

Holy shit. I open my mouth and stick my tongue out like a good girl. Liliana wipes her tail against my tongue, the flavor of Hyacinth bursting on my tongue. Her cum tastes like peaches now that she's in heat. I want to taste more.

Laying Hyacinth on her back I move to her front and dip between her legs. I lap at the delicious taste of her cum, my ass in the air. Liliana rubs at my ass and it sends tingles racing up and down my spine.

She smacks my ass as I eat out Hyacinth's delicious pussy. Our little Human is back to squeezing her own boobs, thrusting against my tongue. Her legs clamp around my head and cut off my breathing as she orgasms around me. I'm surrounded by her and I never want it to end.

Hyacinth's legs are still clamped around me when I feel Liliana's tail probe at my pussy through my clothes.

"These need to come off," she demands at the same time Hyacinth's legs relax around me.

Liliana reaches around my waist, unbuttoning my pants and pulling them down to my knees. She doesn't bother to take them off all the way, her hands spread my ass cheeks as her tail penetrates me.

"Oh, fuck." My eyes roll back in my head as she fucks me mercilessly. My clothes have trapped my legs in this position.

I can feel the otherworldly pleasure of Liliana's powers rushing through my veins now. My pussy clenches harder around her tail and I can't stand the pleasure. It's too intense.

"Please, mommy." I whimper. "Please let me cum."

I scream as she finally lets me, my body collapsing onto the sheets.

"That's my good little witch." She strokes my hair, tenderly. "And how is my little pet?"

Liliana turns to Hyacinth, who is rubbing her clit as she watches us through heavy lids. She pulls Liliana into a kiss and they move so beautifully together. God, I fucking love both of them.

Love?!

It's not just the heat of the moment, I've known for a while that I love my little human. Liliana has surprised me, but I think I love her too. I've never felt more safe and protected. She is the perfect alpha for me and Hyacinth.

I quickly strip off my clothes and move over to them. They are still kissing, hands buried in each other's pussies. I move behind Liliana, kissing and sucking at the spot where her wings meet her back. She buckles against me, but still continues on with Hyacinth. I trail a finger laced with electricity down her spine until I grip the base of her tail.

"Oh fuck, little Witch." Her butt grinds against me, and I take the hint.

I keep my hand wrapped around her tail and stroke back and forth, her hips move in time with me and so do her moans. I continue kissing her back, moving onto her wings and gently placing kisses there too.

Wings and tails can be incredibly sensitive and it doesn't take long before she's flipped around and pushed me onto my back. The whole move is so primal that I gush, my pussy dripping.

My body starts to grow intensely hot, sweat slicking my skin as my vision goes blurry.

"I-it's happening." I tell her quickly before I lose my grip on my sanity.

Chapter 48

L*iliana*

Addison has my full focus, her face is flushed and she's starting to spark. Nothing dangerous, just little bolts escaping her. My hands prickle where they touch her, and I gently stroke her arms just to double check that Hyacinth will be safe.

She clings to me, grinding on my leg and triggering me with her omega whine. The need to pleasure her consumes me, and I kiss down her neck. Gripping her hips, I press her against my leg tighter to increase the friction. She is basically humping my leg at this point, her hips moving quickly as she rides me to completion. I don't control her cumming this time, she needs to get the first one out of her system.

"Please," she whimpers. "Fuck me with your tongue, mommy."

I can't deny her anything right now. I push her onto her back, moving between her legs. But I'm interrupted by a tiny voice coming from behind me.

"Can I call you mommy, too?"

I turn to see Hyacinth sitting upright, brown doe eyes shining in the dim lighting.

"Come here, baby." She crawls to me, and I give her a tender kiss. "Of course you can call me mommy."

I squeeze her ass, pulling her up against my hip.

"Now go kiss your mate while I fuck her with my tongue." I gesture towards Addison's head.

"Yes, mommy." My pussy clenches at her words. She crawls up to Addison and begins to kiss her. They are wrapped in each other as I bend my head back down to my little witch's pussy.

Addison grips one of my horns while Hyacinth grips the other. I can't help my tail moving up to rub at Hyacinth's pussy. My tail fucks her while I shift my tongue to fuck Addison. I can't help but make my tongue and tail vibrate when my mates grip my horns harder. I control all of our pleasure, letting the pressure build up slowly.

I slip my free hand between my legs and rub my clit, the friction is exactly what I need. I manage their pleasure with my powers so that when my orgasm crashes into me, I make sure that they are also cumming all over me.

I'm a drenched, panting mess. My tongue tastes like violets from Addison's cum. I lift my tail to my mouth and lick it, letting the flavor of peaches mix with violets.

My girls are also panting, both of their eyes clear of the haze of lust for now. It seems we have a brief reprieve.

"Hold on, I'll get some things to clean up."

I go to the bathroom, grabbing the wash cloths that we laid out earlier. I soak them and bring them back to the nest with me. I wipe my sleepy girls clean, moving them to a fresher part of the nest. After I clean myself up, I toss the dirty blankets into the hamper and lay out fresh ones.

By the time I'm done with tidying up everything, Hyacinth and Addison are fast asleep and wrapped in each other's arms. They look so peaceful that I can't disturb them.

There's also no chance that I am sleeping right now. I am too on alert, I need to make sure that I keep my mates safe and cared for.

We've been down here for hours, so I go to the kitchen to heat up some food for them.

The microwave buzzes in the background as I mentally run through everything that has occurred. My mates moved so beautifully together. Fuck, they are so incredible.

I can't believe that I am standing here, with two mates resting in our nest. Is this really my life? I feel like I could wake up any moment and this would all be some elaborate dream. It's far too good to be true.

The microwave ding pulls me from my thoughts.

Heading back downstairs, I set the bowls next to the nest and gently wake my girls up with forehead kisses. Their sleepy faces are so adorable, but they act like scavengers when I give them their noodles.

Once we're done eating, I pile some pillows up against the wall that meets the nest in a sort of makeshift headboard and lean up against it, my wings splayed out beneath me. Addison curls up next to me, her head resting on my chest. Hyacinth chooses to put her head on my lap to lay flat. I stroke Addison's arm and Hyacinth's hair as they fall back to sleep.

It doesn't take long before my eyelids are fluttering too, and I decide to take a little rest myself.

Chapter 49

Hyacinth

Being with Addison and Liliana separately was amazing, but having them together is perfection. I feel like the pet that Liliana tells me I am, I'm draped across her lap and practically purring as she scratches my scalp. I could stay here forever in perfect contentment.

My pussy begins to throb again, almost out of nowhere.

"I thought it was over," I say to Liliana as I sit up. I feel like crying, this has been so good but I'm ready for it to be over now.

"Oh, baby." She strokes my cheek. "It's going to be a couple days, remember?"

I'm hot all over again, and I can't help but straddle her leg. Addison stirs next to us, her eyes a lusty haze as she opens them. She pulls me in for a decadent kiss, her plush lips swollen against mine. I feel tender, but the heat doesn't care about that.

Liliana's wings wrap tightly around us when we kiss, completely blocking out the light. I feel her head nudge against mine, and I pull away to kiss her. A moment later and she's kissing Addison too. It's all so very gentle for now, and that's a relief.

I feel lightheaded, and I'm grateful for the food that Liliana brought us before we went to sleep. I'm sure I would have passed out otherwise. Last night was intense, but I wouldn't change a thing.

I feel Liliana's personal brand of pleasure press against my senses. Judging by Addison's moan, so can she.

"You're doing so well, princess." Liliana says against my ear before teasing my lobe between her teeth. It sends a shiver down my neck. I can feel cum leaking from my pussy, Addison is there before I even have to think about it. She rubs at my clit, sending bolts of electricity through me. Addison works me with a mix of pain and pleasure, all while Liliana manages my pleasure, making sure that I linger at the edge of orgasm. It's torturous, but in the best way.

I alternate between kissing them both, still wrapped in Liliana's wings. My hands clench tightly in her hair as Addison sends a really strong bolt straight into my clit. I squeal at the shock and cry out at the same time in ecstasy as Liliana finally allows my nerves to let me cum. I gush, squirting my cum all over the three of us.

My mates cry out too, and I know that Liliana has somehow made sure that they both orgasm. That was the most I have ever felt, and it makes me emotional. Tears stream down my face and I make a pretty audible sniffling noise.

Liliana immediately opens her wings, letting the light in.

"Pet," she gently guides me by my chin to look up at her. "Did we hurt you?"

"N-no," I sniffle some more, unable to stop my tears. "I- that was just..."

"What is it, sweetheart?" Addison strokes my hair. I glance up to see a worried look pass between them.

"I love you." I blurt. "Both of you. I love you both so much, and I- I just have a lot of feelings about that."

"I love you both too." Liliana says, simply.

"I love you, Hyacinth," Addison kisses my head. "I love you too, Liliana."

They share a sweet kiss and I am so happy my heart could burst. It just sends me into a new flood of tears. Addison tears up too, and we both become blubbering messes.

Our horniness comes back in full swing though, and this time our energy is focused on Addison. I kiss and suck on her nipples, alternating between that and kissing her. Liliana licks her clit and fucks her pussy with her tail. With Liliana's help, we all cum together again.

While I am enjoying all these orgasms, I still feel like there is something missing. Like there is something that I need to do.

"Can I talk to you for a second?" I nervously ask. I don't want to bring down the mood, but I know that it's important to communicate.

"Of course, princess. What's up?" Liliana strokes my back and Addison cups my cheek in her hand.

"I am just feeling something, and I don't want to offend either of you." I look between them nervously but they wait for me to continue. "It's just, it feels like something is—no, I don't want to say missing. But it feels like there is something that I'm supposed to do. That I *have* to do."

Liliana

I share a look with Addison, this was inevitable. She nods in silent agreement for me to continue. I hope that this goes well and we don't push Hyacinth away, this is all done so differently for humans.

"We know what it is."

Hyacinth's eyes perk up and she has a hopeful but expectant expression on her face.

"Well, you know how we are mates?" Hyacinth nods, so I continue. "Well, you see, we haven't actually *completed* our bond yet."

"What does that mean?"

"It means that what you're feeling is the need to be claimed by Liliana." Addison explains, stroking Hyacinth's hair gently. "I feel it too. And if we're being honest, our heat might not even finish until she does claim us."

"Then let's do it!" Hyacinth is adorably innocent at times. "My pussy is throbbing, heck, everywhere is. I don't want to be this horny anymore."

"She hasn't explained properly to you what it means to be claimed." I advise, trying to rein in her excitement a little so that I have her focus. This is a big decision for her, one I'm not even sure she is in a fit state to make.

"I would have to bite you." I let my teeth graze her neck, just imagining it makes me unbearably wet. It's so difficult to hold myself back from just biting her now.

"Why do I find the idea of you biting me incredibly erotic?" She looks between me and Addison like it's some crazy thought.

"Mating bites are permanent, Hyacinth. Once I give you my claiming bite, it will always be visible on you. We will always be tied to one another."

"I want to do it." She sounds so sure of her commitment to us both.

Chapter 50

Hyacinth

I know that this bite sounds very serious, and that it's probably a decision that is not to be made lightly. But there is just no way that there is anyone else in this world who is a better fit for me than either of my mates.

And isn't that the whole point of mates, anyway? They are a gift from the universe, and looking at Addison and Liliana, I know that to be true.

"Are you sure?" Liliana checks in with me one last time.

"I'm sure." I grip Addison's hand tightly though.

She has already vocalized that she wants this to happen too. Liliana just needs that push.

"Bite me, mommy."

She laps and kisses at my neck, but she doesn't bite me straight away. Instead, her tail pushes between my legs and she starts to fuck me with it again.

It's not long before I am close to the edge, her tail still inside me now. It's vibrating and pressed up right against my G-spot. The pleasure is overwhelming, my vision going spotty.

"Are you sure you want this, Hyacinth."

"Yes," I pull her into a deep kiss to prove that I mean it. "I love you, Liliana. I want you to claim me."

I want this more than anything, my instincts screaming at me that this is the right thing to do.

She keeps me teetering on that edge for another minute or two, kissing along my neck and collarbone. She pauses right where my neck meets my shoulder.

"You're mine." She growls, and I've never heard that tone in her voice before.

"Yes," I sigh, as her fangs finally sink into me. There is no pain, only pleasure as my orgasm overtakes me.

The connection that forms between us is almost tangible. Liliana laps at the spot, stopping me from bleeding everywhere. Her little licks are so comforting, and she wears such a self-satisfied smile.

Addison

Watching my two mates claim one another is such a privilege. I'm tangled up in their limbs throughout the full process, hands stroking me and including me. Hyacinth keeping a vice-like grip on my hand. I'm not ashamed to say that I spent the whole time with my fingers between my legs. I've worked myself up into a frenzy, the need to orgasm so strong.

All I want now is to be claimed by my alpha. For her to make me cum as her fangs sink into me.

"Please," I can't help but whimper.

Liliana switches places with me, so that I am pressed against the pile of pillows and cushions. They're comforting against me, and thankfully cool to the touch. Hyacinth settles herself in between my legs, her tongue darting out to lick my clit. It feels so good and it's such a struggle to not just grab her by the hair and suffocate her there. I fist her curls anyway, a shiver passing through me at the delicate touch of her tongue.

Liliana pulls me in for a kiss, and it is so tender and loving. She lovingly tugs on my lip with her teeth as she pulls away.

"Are you sure that you want this?" Her eyes search mine intently.

"Yes. I—" I need a second as a particularly sweet wave of pleasure washes over me as Hyacinth still works my pussy. "I want you to claim me, alpha."

Liliana strikes my neck, and I cum so hard that I really do black out for a minute.

Liliana

Addison loses consciousness for a moment, and I'm worried that I pushed her too far. I should have claimed them earlier in their heats. For their first time, I am sure this has been a lot. But I wanted them to come to me, to beg me for it.

She comes back to us quickly. Myself and Hyacinth are both hovering over her with concern. But she just smiles as she opens her violet eyes.

"My mates." Addison states. It feels so right to hear her say that.

We all tear up a little bit, tangled in each other's arms in a way that we will never be able to recreate.

I have never felt this whole before.

Life as a succubus has felt pretty lonely up until now. But I will never be alone again.

Leaning into Hyacinth's neck, I lick and kiss at her mating mark before doing the same to Addison. Knowing that I placed those marks there is the most satisfying feeling. They're *mine*.

Having my omegas tucked into my arms is everything that I have ever wanted.

Even though things were a bit difficult at times in the journey to get here, I know in my soul that it has all led me to this moment.

I feel complete. This is the path that we are supposed to be on, I feel so grateful that I have them both.

Epilogue

H*yacinth*

Six Months Later

The doorbell rings right as I am taking the cookies out of the oven.

"Just a second!" I call, setting down the pan and switching off the oven. I slip off my oven mitts as I walk to the door. There's a flash of crimson through the glass panel. Why was Liliana ringing the doorbell?

I quickly open the door and I can't help but bust out in laughter at the sight before me. Liliana is covered in mud with little Pippa shivering in her arms, also covered in mud.

"What happened?"

"Let us in please and I will tell you from the bathtub."

I stand in the doorway of the bathroom as Liliana cleans Pippa, our tiny Chihuahua puppy. Once we have a clean pup, I gather her up in a fluffy towel and hold her close. I always thought it was a myth that tiny dogs shivered constantly. But Pip was proving that they are in fact in a constant state of shake.

Liliana finally got her pet when we moved in together and I brought Alfred along with me. However, it wasn't long after she realized that you couldn't exactly pet frogs whenever you wanted that she decided Alfred needed a sister.

Addison is usually more of a cat person, but when we visited the shelter we just knew that Pippa was ours.

Liliana strips off, dumping her clothes in the hamper and rinsing and filling the bath for herself. She tells me about the massive truck that drove through an impressive puddle to cover her and our tiny dog.

"Ooh, is it bath time?!" Addison squeals, rushing into the bathroom. She quickly strips her clothes and gets into the bath with Liliana. I set Pippa on the floor with her towel, adding another to her pile. She immediately goes nuts, huffing and rubbing her little nose and body against them.

Stripping off my own clothes, I join my mates in our tub. Addison is already cozied up next to Liliana on one side, so I head for her other.

One nice thing about monster built houses is how big the bathtubs are. Oh, and the beds are also enormous and so comfy.

We stayed in Addison's house for a while after being mated. But my mates were getting more and more anxious about me staying there. They weren't comfortable with me going outside on my own.

So Addison bought us a house not too far from Flora and Sebastian, which is so useful for work, but also just to hang out with our friends.

Speaking of work, when Sebastian and Flora signed up to their next few albums with the label, Addison obviously knew she would be working on them. But it was a total surprise to me that one of the condition's to Flora's contract is that I stay on to work on her albums, too. And with Flora and Sebastian's new collab album coming up soon, Addison and I are currently working together on it.

Liliana is doing pretty great at work too. Now that she has resolved things with Sebastian, the label has been so much more supportive of her. She was promoted and given a pay rise.

With Flora and Sebastian going on tour in a few weeks, Addison and I would both have had a lot of time off work. Fortune Record's solution to this is to have us try and work with another artist. I'm a bit worried about how that is going to go, because it's with Ivy on her next album. Judging by how much she frustrated Liliana... we're going to either love or hate working with her.

I stretch across Liliana and kiss Addison before turning back to my alpha.

"I love you both so much."

I snuggle back into my alpha's arms, next to my omega mate, and I can't help but feel so much joy with how everything turned out.

The Zodiac Society

If you enjoyed this book, try out some of my other stories... Month one is free on my Patreon.

Twelve signs. Twelve creatures. One challenge that could change everything.

When a freshman astronomy student stumbles into a nightclub that doesn't exist on any map, she's not looking for magic. She's looking for somewhere—anywhere—to disappear. But what she finds instead is a shimmering pocket of enchantment hidden on campus: the Zodiac Society.

By morning, she's waking up in Zodiac House with a choice—forget what she saw and go back to her ordinary life, or take the Zodiac Challenge: seduce twelve paranormals aligned with the signs of the zodiac, and earn her place in the Society. The rules are outrageous. The reward? Power, freedom, and a new name: Astraea.

Her first assignment? Aries.

Blaze is a faun with smoldering eyes, a sadistic streak, and a taste for control. His element is fire—and he knows exactly how to wield it. In a night of sharp pain and blistering pleasure, Astraea is stripped down, opened up, and set ablaze—inside and out. She's never submitted to anyone before. She never knew she could.

But this challenge is more than a string of pleasure-filled encounters. As Astraea dives into this world of monsters, magic, and illicit seduction, she begins to feel a pull toward something deeper—especially from the three Society members tasked with guiding her through the challenge: cool, clever Winslow; golden-hearted Ellis; and commanding, mysterious Miles.

And beneath it all, her body is changing. Her senses are sharpening. Something inside her is waking up.

Astraea might have entered the Zodiac Society by accident. But she's not leaving by choice.

ARIES is a high-heat, monster romance novella set in a secret society of pleasure, magic, and transformation. Each novella in The Zodiac Society series features a new zodiac-inspired creature, a spicy standalone seduction arc, and a slow-burning emotional journey that culminates in a shared HEA.

You will receive a new short story, exclusive artwork, and a page straight from Astraea's secret journal every month!

A Note from Sofia

Thank you so much for deciding to pick up my book!

I write across the paranormal and omegaverse romance genres, please check out my other books if that interests you.

To stay in the loop, scan the QR code for my important links, or go to https://sofiaroseauthor.com/

To be updated of even more news, consider signing up to my newsletter on my website.

Aster

A MONSTER FFF ROMANCE

A buttoned-up human sound tech. A powerful alpha succubus. A soft-hearted witch. One music label, two tempting monsters... and a whole lot of feelings Hyacinth wasn't expecting.

Hyacinth knows monsters exist. She's just never had to work with them.

As the newest tech at Fortune Records, she's determined to keep her head down, her wires tidy, and her hor-